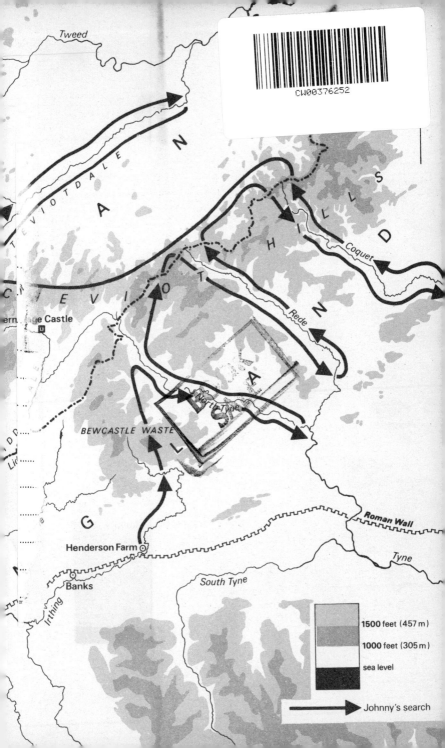

Tweed

CW00376252

TEVIOTDALE

CHEVIOT

C

ern...ge Castle

HILLS

D

Coquet

Rede

N

T

A

North Tyne

S

BEWCASTLE WASTE

L

Roman Wall

G

Henderson Farm

Banks

South Tyne

Tyne

Irthing

1500 feet (457 m)

1000 feet (305 m)

sea level

Johnny's search

Reivers' Weather

'Our causes are something alike, Johnny,' Rainault the minstrel had said, as together they watched the swift tide of the Solway Firth. And so, indeed, they were—both boys seeking revenge for a sister dishonoured, in the wild lands of the Border at the turn of the sixteenth century.

Neither Johnny nor Rainault expected to exact full vengeance from the great men of other clans whom they pursued, yet to yield would have been unquestionable, and to consider the consequences of their actions entirely alien to the principles of that colourful, barbaric society.

Also by Molly Holden

*

A TENANCY OF FLINT
WHITE ROSE AND WANDERER

Reivers' Weather

By

Molly Holden

CHATTO & WINDUS · LONDON

Published by
Chatto & Windus Ltd.
40 William IV Street
London WC2

652536

JF

ISBN 0 7011 5024 6

Printed in Great Britain by
T. & A. Constable Ltd
Hopetoun Street, Edinburgh

Contents

CHAPTER 1

The raid

There cam' a wind frae out the north,
A cauld wind and a snell . . .

A STORM of mingled heavy rain and wet snow swept over the fells as Johnny came across the yard with a pitch-fork full of hay for the cows in the byre. The wind, a fierce north-easterly, was behind him; he met Jock struggling into the storm to fetch a second load of last summer's sweetness to feed the winter beasts. The little man was drenched but cheerful, red hair blown across his eyes, head half-down but the smile clear on his cold-bitten features.

'Reivers' weather,' he shouted to Johnny in passing.

Johnny only grunted in reply. It was indeed in such weather that the raiders had used to descend on farm-steads; but the Border had been quiet enough for some ten years now, since the King of Scotland had become also the King of England and had tamed the foraying society of his borders with some ferocity. Jock remembered the raids well enough; Johnny, at seventeen, could barely do so although it was in one of the last such raids that his own father had been killed, in retaliation for some expedition of his own. So far as Johnny knew, all had been fair recompense, nothing more had come of it. Though some-times, on winter evenings in the firelight, Hugh, an old raiding companion of Johnny's father who had been dragged from that last fight crippled and half-blind and now lived on here on the family's hospitality, would grumble and groan about the failure to take revenge.

Johnny's mother always hushed him; she would have no talk of warfare now. Johnny had been only seven at the time of his father's death. He remembered little of that black day.

And was not interested now. He did his duty as eldest son, keeping the farm going although his heart was not in farming; so he had only grunted at Jock's remark, going forward with the wind, his auburn-gold hair blown wet around his face. He thought no more about it.

Half an hour later he remembered the saying, cursing that he had not set lookouts as he should have done—it was still not wise to be too trusting. For a group of riders —young men mounted on the sturdy, cobby horses of the Border country—came shouting in at the unbarred eastern gate, the storm at their backs so that it blew into the farm people's faces.

It was not, at first, too earnest a raid, for some of the attackers, no older than Johnny, were laughing at the surprise that they had caused and there were no weapons in evidence. They sought cattle though. That must be resisted, for cattle were even more precious in winter than at other times. However, the raiders might have been driven off with no more than fierce blows and exchanged insults had not Hugh, that great gaunt man dragging his crippled leg behind him, appeared at the door of the tower, long sword in hand, his eyes alight with the lust for blood, so long repressed, shouting forgotten names and old battle-cries.

Johnny, hanging on to the halter of his best winter heifer, not daring to loose hold even for an instant to snatch his knife from his belt and use it on the tall boy on a strong horse who was dragging the heifer away, cursed the appearance of Hugh, fond as he was of him. His presence accelerated the fight, as Johnny had guessed it would. Knives and swords began to flash among the

whirling snow. Johnny's opponent himself drew out again
the knife that he had used to sever the heifer's tether and
Johnny felt the blow in his right shoulder as the tall boy
stooped from his horse and struck. The force of the blow
sent Johnny staggering back. He caught his foot in piles
of hay put ready by the byre, fell on the wounded shoulder,
and fierce pain, felt for the first time, blackened his eye-
sight and deprived him of his senses.

A lull came in the storm. Hugh was still fighting like a
madman and shouting obscenities at a few armed men
incensed by his words. He was out in the yard now. The
other fighting was scattered and sporadic—there were not
many men in this homestead. Already some of the cattle
were being led away.

A girl came from the door of the lower tower that Hugh
had left ajar. The women were forbidden out in such circumstances but she stood there bravely, clenching her
fists in fury at her inability to help. Jock, crouched in the
lee of the byre, holding his head, which was aching from
a heavy blow, glanced up and saw her and chuckled to
himself. Trust Johnny's sister to want to be part of any
family affair. Then, in that same lull in the storm, he saw
a rider, a dark-golden boy, sweep round the courtyard and
check his horse at sight of Helen. Jock saw them stare at
each other almost as if there were mutual recognition.
Then, as the boy urged his horse nearer the tower door,
the wet snow swept down again and Jock, cursing, staggering to his feet to give Helen any protection he could, saw
no more. He could only guess that the rider had bent and
swept the not-unwilling girl into his arms and on to his
saddle and made for the gates.

The affray ebbed. The storm began to clear away to the
west and Johnny, coming to his senses again, saw that
several cattle were missing. He got to his feet, angry,
feeling guilty also for having been taken so by surprise,

and saw Hugh on his hands and knees in the slush of the yard, alone. Weak with the violent loss of blood, Johnny swayed to him and knelt to support him.

'Hendersons,' gasped Hugh, and retched blood horribly. 'I kenned the sons, for all my sight. Their father slew yours, Johnny. Take revenge, take revenge.'

He fell forward into the trampled snow, brown with mud and blood. Johnny crouched above his body, dazed with shock.

When Jock approached him and laid a hand on his shoulder, saying urgently: 'We maun look for Helen, lad,' he did not reply. He did not, in truth, hear what Jock was saying. He only saw Hugh's blood fresh on the snow but darkening now, merging with the other muck of battle, and had dim memories of times he could not have known, and felt obligations laid on him that he did not wish to accept.

Chapter 2

A matter of honour

. . . take better care o' your youngest sister
For your eldest's awa the last night.

AFTERWARDS—all the gates barred and lookouts set—
Johnny, nursing his bound and pulling shoulder in the
smoky hall, found obligations that he accepted instantly.
He had recovered somewhat from the shock of Hugh's
death and now heard Jock telling again of Helen's
probable abduction. This time he heard the story clearly.

Jock was a hard-headed man but he said something
that every man in the hall—save Johnny in his fury—
recognised as possibility or truth, for all their unsenti-
mental Border heads and hearts. 'I think 'twas love at
first sight between herself an' the one who took her,' he
said, surprisingly. 'I kenned the look o' it from long ago.'
He chuckled.

Johnny's mother sighed. 'Better so,' she said. 'She'll
no be unhappy, maybe.'

Johnny stood up, furiously, his head swimming. 'We've
to find her,' he said, 'an' bring her back. She is our
honour.'

His mother looked across the crowded hall at him, her
handsome, angry, eldest son standing there in the firelight
with the blood high in his cheeks; her heart turned for
him, and for her first child, the snatched daughter. But
she said: 'Your first duty is here, Johnny, to your home.
Jamie is yet too young to take over the farm. An' your
shoulder must mend.'

Johnny stared at her, glanced at his fifteen-year-old brother, then at Jock (but knowing that there could be no question of Jock's taking over the farm, it must stay in family hands), then stared at his mother again.

'Do ye no want to find her?' he asked harshly. 'She'll be passed from man to man along the Border, like as no, an' there's our honour gone.'

'Nay,' said Jock, surprisingly again, mildly, 'I think no, lad. There was no anyone else for him any more than for her by that look I saw. He'll no let her go.'

Johnny glared at him. 'I dinna believe it,' he said. 'An' it's no your honour in question, Jock.'

Johnny's mother said: '*Your* honour is here, Johnny, for the while at least.'

She was a gentle woman, very like her eldest son in looks—the same ashen-auburn hair with the same rough wave in it, the fair skin, the clear grey eyes—in poor health since the death of her husband and the posthumous birth of her last child. This was the fair-faced, ten-year-old Griselda who gazed in bewilderment round the hall now at the harsh, surprising words. She adored her eldest brother; he hardly noticed her existence.

There was another son, Thomas, older than Griselda by almost two years, and he understood more of what was happening this evening. His mother noticed, with a sinking of the heart, that his expression was as pugnacious as Johnny's. This was the full tally of that fatherless family —the girl gone, the angry eldest boy, the silent middle son, a daughter born and dead within a year of Jamie's birth, and the younger brother and sister.

Their mother had spoken clearly and firmly and not words that Johnny wished to accept; yet he said no more for the moment.

That evening though, as mother and son stood in the small chill room that an ancestor had built as a chapel where Hugh's body, now cleaned and quiet, lay on a stone bier, Johnny said: 'I must go seek her, mother, when ye say I may.' If his words were as dutiful as they ought to be, his heart was not.

His mother knew this well enough. She glanced at him, smiling a little. 'Did I bring forth a man o' blood in ye, Johnny, like your father, like Hugh yonder?' She nodded at the dead man.

Johnny swallowed. Then he said, quietly but with anger: 'They will mock our name the length o' the Border an I make no move to defend it.'

In truth, he and his mother were alike in more than looks; it was only the difference between man and woman that made him more careful of honour as she was more careful of happiness. And, for all his short temper, he was not in fact a man of blood, though his mother was yet to realise this. She had come, as a girl, from south of the Wall, to marry Johnny's father—a charmer despite his way of life, and a good landowner and farmer despite his tendency to blood-letting. Her Celtic ancestors and kindred put as great an emphasis on personal honour as had her husband and his Border clan; Johnny inherited from both sides.

But his mother sighed now. 'Is Helen no more to ye than that?' she asked. 'Naught but the family name?'

Johnny was silent, thinking of the dark, lively girl with whom he had grown up and played and quarrelled but whom he loved dearly.

His mother sighed again, turning from the icy room towards the warm hall once more. 'Let your shoulder mend a little, boy,' she said, 'an' ye shall go. Jamie's growing. Jock will help him.'

She left the room, leaving Johnny to stare at the blueing corpse of the man who had fed his youth with tales of battle, raid, and glory. He had never had any great desire to emulate Hugh, though his blood was stirred by the high accounts and the ballads. He did not care to fight for the sake of fighting. But if the matter of honour came up, or a just cause were threatened, he would fight; also, of course, for his livelihood, as he had that afternoon. All that he had in mind at the moment, though, was to set out in search of a beloved sister and to save her from what might be an infamous fate that would be the shame of them all if not prevented, or avenged. A sister debauched was indeed a blot on a family name; he would slay if need be in this cause. But the feeling that he must search for Helen arose also out of a sense of guilt in him, an acknowledgement of responsibility for that unkept watch that had let the raiders in, to take his cattle and his sister. He must discover what had become of her. Jock's soft and surprising words had proved nothing.

*　　*　　*

In the winter weather his wound was slow to heal; it had been deep and viciously dealt. He felt its dull ache every snowy morning on these high fells and knew that his arm was not yet strong enough to raise in revenge. The knowledge irked him. Another feeling troubled him also; he longed to be away for the very sake of travelling. He had felt it before sometimes, but vaguely, not as a pressing need like this. He did not recognise the feeling for the itch of wanderlust that it was.

He watched the farm dutifully for these months. In the spring he would buy in more good cattle if he could; the stock had been hardy and well-known. Jock and Jamie could soon build it up again after the depredations of the raid, if he bought wisely and well. He watched his brother growing, both in strength and sense of responsibility; Jamie was sixteen before the snows began to shrink a little from the fell-tops and the streams began to fill and run faster. He would manage the farm well enough now, Johnny saw. And still the older brother's shoulder bit and ached.

' 'Twill grow no better wi' waiting,' he told himself impatiently. He had his mother look at it.

She had skilful fingers which probed deeply. He could not prevent himself wincing. She looked at him keenly.

'The skin has healed,' she said. 'Ye'll hae seen that for yourself. I canna be sure about the deeper flesh but I think no, yet.'

'It will hae to do,' said Johnny violently. He thanked his mother and pulled his shirt and jacket back brusquely over the scarred shoulder, and belted his dirty sheepskin coat around him again. The winds still blew cold up here on the old Roman Wall ridge and pierced men shrewdly although new green was beginning to show down in the valleys.

Four days later, though, spring seemed to have come to the tops too. The sun shone and although it was not yet strong there was warmth in it. The eternal wind still blew but it was from the west now, no longer the north-east. Johnny sniffed the air, saw the fresh green showing on the steep banks, and decided to go downhill to the valley market for more animals.

He took Jamie, another man, and two of the herding dogs. It was more than a day's journey; the return was particularly slow, driving the plodding beasts, with the black-and-white dogs circling behind the hooves, forever ready to nip when needed, cringing like all their kind when called off for unduly harassing the slow herd.

Johnny stood by the byre that evening, assessing his purchases. Although not fond of farming, he had an eye for a good animal and these cattle, though scant of flesh after their winter rations, were well-boned and would soon make good additions to the farm's herd. They ate, he noticed with satisfaction, with excellent appetites.

He was standing quietly, legs astride, hands on his hips, watching the cattle, when a stranger came up to him, one of the beggars who were travelling the high ways again now that the better weather had come, and were given hospitality at every homestead.

This man was old, grey-haired, bent with the rheumatism of many years' cold and wet travelling. His faded blue eyes were shrewd, however.

He said to Johnny, startling him from a day-dream: 'Are ye he that men call Johnny Armstrong o' Banks?'

Johnny turned. 'Unless there is another wi' the same title,' he said, smiling at the old man, 'I am he. Why do ye ask, father? Ye are welcome, whatever the name o' the place or the people.'

'Aye, I ken that, lad,' said the old beggar. 'But if ye are he, an' lost a sister in a raid at the start o' the winter' —he paused, seeing Johnny's eyes flicker in admission of this fact—'then I hae a message for ye.'

Johnny waited, his heart thumping. He saw that he could not hurry the old man.

'I was to say,' went on the beggar, 'as if the message were straight from Helen—would that be the name?' Johnny nodded, less patient now. 'I am safe an' well an' happy. It were best that ye forget ye ever had an elder sister.'

The old man was no gossip but he experienced the natural delight of the messenger who brings unexpected news as he saw Johnny's eyes widen at him.

'Where did ye get that message?' demanded Johnny, seizing his shoulder, 'who gave it ye?'

'Nay,' said the old man, freeing himself and turning away a little. 'I hae no more to tell ye, young man. The message was passed by an acquaintance to the east o' here who learned that I would be travelling this way. Where it came from to him, I dinna ken. Take it or leave it, as ye see fit.'

Johnny felt in his pocket for a silver groat for the old man. As he passed it to him, he said pleadingly: 'Tell me where the message was passed to ye.'

The old man inclined his head in thanks as he took the alms. Then he looked at Johnny with kindly as well as shrewd eyes. 'She said no to go looking for her,' he said. 'Leave well alone, laddie.'

Johnny shook his head. 'I must seek her out,' he said. 'I swore I would when she was taken. But I was hurt an' there was the farm to tend. A man told me the reivers were Hendersons.'

The old man looked into the boy's face. At last he said reluctantly: ' 'Twas there I got the news. But the lad who gave it me came from farther north or west. She was no in that homestead, I ken.'

Johnny thanked him and was turning slowly away. Suddenly he turned back: 'Ye could tell me o' what like was this messenger,' he said abruptly.

Again the old man paused. Then he said slowly, 'A minstrel. Young. Dark. Like—like a flame.'

The words surprised Johnny, then he assumed that the old man meant to describe only the conventional colours of a minstrel's costume—red, gold, blue.

'Ye can tell me more, father,' he said pleadingly.

The old man looked into his urgent face, and softened. 'I mind me he had a foreign-sounding name but I forget it. He was no a man o' this island. Truly, I can tell ye no more.'

Johnny thanked him again, seeing that this was indeed so, now. As he turned away, the old man touched his arm. 'If she's happy, that's a' that matters, lad,' he said gently.

But Johnny shook his head and would not reply. He would start his search within the week, he told himself.

B

CHAPTER 3

Restlessness

O the wind is longer nor the way
And love is deeper nor the sea . . .

THE next morning Johnny, accompanied by his hunting dogs, strolled out of the encircling walls of the homestead to look at the pasture and judge how soon he could let the cattle out to graze on fresh grass. It was growing well. He kicked at a tuft or two with a booted foot, absent-mindedly, and then turned, some hundred yards along the ridge, to look back at his home, without really being aware that he was doing so.

Although he had lived there all his life he felt no great regret at the thought of leaving it soon in his search for Helen.

The buildings were set to the south of the considerable height that remained of the Roman Wall, that had once snaked along the whole ridge of these hills in the north of England; it was here used as one of the outer defences of the courtyard. The men and women who lived hereabouts, near the western seaboard, spoke of the district as the Wall or the Border indiscriminately—it was still something of the debatable land that it had been in times past, for all the recent peace. To the south of the Wall, men and women thought of themselves as English and some of the folk to the north did so also. But, beyond the Border which ran to the north-east from here, north of the Cheviot Hills, all were Scots, however like the English they might be in speech or dress. Few people knew anything of the very different Highland Scots much further north. But even now, with peace official, nationality still mattered less than the old tradition of feuding between families; so that these Armstrongs, to the south of the Border, cared nothing for their wilder cousins north of the Border in Liddesdale and had been only concerned with their enmity with the Hendersons and Crozers, not many valleys away.

Johnny's farm was known as Banks because of the many great ditches and ramparts around—remnants perhaps of a fort even older than the Roman Wall which had been robbed in so many places to build such homesteads. But here the Wall stood twenty feet tall, protection for the little settlement from weather and enemies from the north. The main building was the peel-tower, only two storeys high, nothing grand like the gaunt towers of the great families; the ground floor was for storage, curving stone stairs that could be easily defended led to the living-room above. Around it had been built, at various times, byres and stables. It looked almost cosy this morning, as far as any buildings on such uplands could look cosy; his mother had had the inner walls of the courtyard limewashed and they caught whatever sun there was, at any time of year, however briefly.

So Johnny looked at it detachedly, the thatched roofs with the great stones slung across them to hold them down against winter gales, the stack of the last hay of last year within the yard, the night's damp steaming from stone walls and tiles in the early sunlight. To his left and south the ground dropped sharply several hundred feet, to his pastures and hayfields, to the glittering stream that watered his cattle. To his right, beyond the Wall, lay rougher uplands with only a little true pasture among them.

Johnny did not see it as a desolate land to farm. He knew nothing of land in which men farmed under kinder conditions. This was his lot; he might not care for it greatly but he knew no choice.

He began to walk slowly back toward the eastern gates. They were open and apparently undefended but Johnny had learned from the raid that someone must always have an eye to all who approached. Jock was at work nearest the gates this morning; he saw, in his capacity as lookout, Johnny's approach, and lifted a welcoming hand. Johnny nodded acknowledgement. He was not much given to demonstration of any sort, as his mother knew, to her occasional sadness. His feelings might be deep and passionate but were only really in evidence when he lost his temper —a not so infrequent occurrence. His mother had always feared that some mischance might occur, to himself or to others, in these fits of rage.

He put the cattle out to grass that noon, when the sun was warm; and every day after that for four days in the flash of spring. By the end of even that short time the difference in their coats and their weight was startlingly apparent.

'Ye bought well there, Johnny,' nodded Jock in approval as they stood to watch the herd one evening.

'I think so,' said Johnny, his curt manner concealing the pleasure he felt at Jock's praise. And he knew he could leave the herd, the farm, the summer harvesting in Jock's hands and in the increasingly competent hands of Jamie. He went to find his mother and tell her of his intention to leave the next morning.

She saw the expression on his face as he entered the hall and began to cross to where she sat. She stood, and moved towards him, so that they stood alone by the fireplace. He said: 'I can go now, mother. I can see that the farm will be well.'

She said, through pale lips: 'Even without my permission, Johnny?'

He flung a hand sideways impatiently. 'Ah!' he said. 'Give it me, mother. I must go while the trail is still something fresh. I've waited overlong. I must go anyway.'

She, torn between love of son and daughter, saw that he would indeed go anyway. She asked: 'What evidence have ye, Johnny? What trail?'

He had not told her of the beggar's words. He did so now, as near as to what was actually said as he could remember, for Johnny, whatever his faults, was honest.

He saw her hesitating. 'If those are truly Helen's words,' she said at last, 'we disregard her wishes to track her down.'

Her son's face hardened. 'I must find out,' he said. 'I'll no take reported words like that for gospel truth. I'll see for myself where honour and dishonour lie.'

There was no arguing with him. His mother touched his shoulder softly. 'Go with my blessing, son,' she said. 'But oh, if ye should find her and all is well, do no break her life.'

He muttered something, lowering his head.

Chapter 4

The journey begins

He's mounted on his berry-brown steed,
And merry, merry rade he on . . .

WHEN Johnny set out next morning, he had no very
clear idea in his mind as to what he would do. His pride
would not allow him to travel in disguise to his enemy's
territory so he wore his usual good home-spun shirt and
breeches of Lodden grey and, over these, the quilted
leather jacket interlined with squares of horn as a protection in battle. If the Border was formally at peace, yet
men still took no chances. His father's jacket of this sort
had been too slashed and blood-stained to be saved and
handed on to him. He remembered, with a slight pang of
conscience, his mother and Helen sewing this new jacket,
stabbing the strong leather with long needles in the slow
process of making, lining, and interlining. If he outgrew
this, or, indeed, if he came back at all, it would be handed
down to Jamie, and another made. Rolled in his saddlebag, he carried a good grey cloak for extra warmth, and
provisions for several days. For arms, he carried only the
dagger in his belt, the sword at his side; and he rode his
own good horse. He went openly and would have thought
the less of himself if he had not.

His first objective was the Henderson farm which he
knew lay a day's ride to the east. How he would approach
or enter it he had not the least idea, how announce himself
or behave to the Hendersons themselves. He had no
thoughts of revenge either for his father or Hugh or even

for the cattle-stealing. His sole idea for the moment was to attempt to trace back the movements of the vagrant who had given Helen's message to the old beggar, if indeed it was truly a message from Helen. The task seemed almost impossible; even Johnny, from the seclusion of his farm, realised how wide the Border was and the Marches of England and Scotland either side, and how many vagrants and broken men wandered its length and breadth.

It was a morning of sun and cloud shadow from the north-west as he had set out. The yard had been busy. All had known where he was going and had given him a brief 'good luck'. None expected to see him again. Even his mother had resigned herself to this. She had bidden him farewell in her bower, away from the rest of the household, murmuring a blessing against his forehead as he bent on one knee to her and she kissed him. So many mothers had lost and still lost sons in quarrels along the Border that she could scarcely hope for better luck herself.

As Johnny rose, she had suddenly whispered something very surprising, but as if on impulse: 'Travel for me, Johnny.'

He had stared at her, completely bewildered by her words. As she saw the question in his face, she had half-laughed at herself and gestured quickly. 'I shouldna hae said that,' she had said. 'Ye'll no understand, child. 'Twas just that I too hae always wished to travel. And I wasna always a sick woman.'

Johnny had lowered his eyes and did not even have the grace to mutter an acknowledgement of this astonishing confidence from his mother. She had smiled ruefully as she looked at him. ' 'Tis no for a lass to do as she pleases,' she said, as if to herself, and with some bitterness. 'But I ken that ye're no loth to go, Johnny. Helen is your plea and danger may be your portion, but I ken somewhat o' ye, boy, for ye are as much me as ye are your father. I'll think on ye.'

She had turned away, proudly erect. Johnny, glancing cautiously at her, had seen tears in her eyes. He had wondered, fleetingly, and with amazement, for whom she wept. He had been aware of his mother as an individual, for the first time in his life. Neither had he ever seen any-one else thus before. But, although he had left the room in a stunned silence as she gestured him away, he soon forgot that revelatory glimpse.

Jock had come by his side to the gate and there clasped hands and parted, calling back the dogs that whined to go with their master but must not on this journey. He had promised Johnny that he would do his best for the farm and Johnny knew he would keep his word.

*   *   *

For the first mile or two, Johnny enjoyed the morning. He rode, though he did not know it, on the old supply road of the Romans, a track to the south of the Wall. The Wall lay on higher land here, black even in the sunlight, grit and granite, with sparse grass bowing to the wind in long grey waves. The river lay far down below to his right, flaked with brilliant reflections this morning as its brown water broke fast and shallow over its pebbled bed. The sky was filled with bright clouds and the ground with their following shadows. It was a good ride in good riding country.

But after the exhilaration of the first few miles, doubts began to rise in Johnny's mind. If he had not considered any plans for his own future conduct, neither had he con-sidered how the Hendersons might greet him. Looking at the situation honestly, he did not foresee any very warm welcome. Even a slight doubt as to whether Helen's fate should come first with him arose. That he dismissed easily; the search for her *must* come first, for honour's sake, even if there were other matters to be dealt with afterwards— such as the small account for stolen cattle!

So he rode the rest of the morning and some of the short afternoon with less enjoyment in the physical act and atmosphere. A short fierce shower of stinging rain and a little hail in the heart of one of the blacker clouds racing overhead forced him up on to the higher land with his cloak pulled close around him to obtain some little shelter from the Wall, which here stood high and firm. Few bothered to rob its stones for building in this cold and starving stretch of land. Yet thieves and clanless men lurked in the ruins of the Roman forts and he kept his wits about him and a good lookout and his hand on his sword-hilt.

Only where the river curved to its head-waters and had gouged a warmer valley out, did the Wall lose height and the wind drop and the sight of a tower and buildings about it below him remind him of farms and quieter folk and then of the Hendersons.

He reined in for a moment, considering. How should he approach the homestead? Again he touched the hilt of his sword; then he decided and rode down.

His shadow ran long before him now as the afternoon drew to its close. The last low rays of the sun touched the western gates of this place and he realised, with a twinge of conscience—an uncomfortable emotion for him—that they kept better watch here than he had set that winter afternoon. A voice called from above the gates to ask his name and business. He reined in again on the flat land before the gates—good pasture, he saw, for cattle recently driven in for safety for the night.

He called back: 'Johnny Armstrong o' Banks, come in peace to seek news o' his sister.'

There was a stunned silence. The open answer had surprised whoever was on guard. Then the voice said: 'Wait
ye a while.'

Johnny sat on his horse patiently enough, glancing
round at the pastures. This was good land, lower than his
own. He felt some anger that they had thought it worth
while to rob his poorer farmstead of its best beasts. Then
he thought: leave that, leave that for now.

The gates were flung back. A tall man—Henderson himself, Johnny guessed—stood there, facing the last dazzle
of light, and called to Johnny to enter. He was as red as
a fox, even allowing for the brilliance of the low rays upon
him; he had a full, curly, square-cut beard, and a broken
nose which gave him a villainous appearance at odds with
the fashionable beard. His red-brown eyes were shrewd
but not unfriendly. He was a man of undeniable presence.

As Johnny started to urge his horse forward with a
pressure of his knees, several young men came about their
father as guard.

He gestured impatiently and walked forward alone
across the tussocked, slant-shadowed grass to greet his
visitor. 'Let there be no ill blood between us, lad,' he said.

Johnny was surprised, yet saw that the greeting seemed
genuine. He nodded back. 'There shall be none now,' he
said.

The older man did not yet stand back and Johnny's
horse waited.

'The cattle raid was none o' my doing,' he said, again
to Johnny's great surprise. 'I was awa'. My young hot-
heads had the making o' that, with a cousin o' theirs
staying.'

'But ye kept the cattle,' observed Johnny sardonically.

'Aye,' agreed Henderson, with a dour grin, acknowledging the hit, 'I kept the cattle. Ye sent none for them,
Armstrong.'

'There was none to send,' replied Johnny curtly. 'We are few men an' those were hurt. And ye kept my sister?'

This was more of a manoeuvre than a question. He was almost sure that Helen was not there.

Henderson shook his head. 'Nay, lad, nay,' he said. 'I would hae sent *her* back. But the situation was a mite confused. Come ye in. I'll tell ye more.'

He stood aside and Johnny's horse, scenting warmth and food and shelter from the quick-coming, chill, spring night, began to move again. Johnny did not check him. He might learn more than he had thought to; it was strange to enter enemy territory thus, though. Vaguely he remembered Hugh's curses upon the Hendersons.

He looked at the sons as he came upon them. He recognised the tall boy with whom he had struggled for the heifer and who had knifed him. His shoulder throbbed at the recollection. The tall boy turned away, affecting indifference. Torches were brought and all was pleasant confusion.

CHAPTER 5

Enemies and friends

. . . But he has keepit his own true love,
Saying 'We'll wauk the woods our lane.'

In the hall, some half-hour later, it was time for the evening meal and Johnny was taken in hand by the youngest Henderson son, a fair cheerful boy of fourteen who announced that his name was Wat and who behaved in a friendly fashion. Johnny sat beside him at table and learned that there were five Henderson sons and that his tall adversary was named Sim. He watched Sim occasionally in the torchlight and saw that Sim was watching him, with a supercilious grin that Johnny would have liked to have wiped from his face.

Wat said blithely: 'Sim doesna like ye.'

'The feeling's o' both sides,' growled Johnny.

'He wanted your sister,' went on Wat gaily, 'but Sander said him nay.'

Johnny turned quickly. 'Who is Sander?' he demanded. The name was strange.

Wat chewed bread. 'Sander?' he said, through a full mouth. 'Alexander. Our cousin. *He* brought her back. I liked her. He's awa' home again now an' she went wi' him.'

Johnny groaned. He remembered Jock telling of the confrontation between Helen and the young man. Had she indeed gone as concubine to some distant cousin of the Hendersons, in a far land? And had she been taken by force, or gone reluctantly, or of her own free will?

He could eat no more nor ask any more questions. He sat back from the board.

As the remains of the meal were cleared away and the tables removed and men mingled freely on the wide warm floor, Johnny suddenly found Sim at his side.

'*I* would think it shame to take bread at my enemy's table,' said the young Henderson mockingly, '*or* to speak wi' a man who had killed *my* father.'

Johnny turned on him furiously. 'That's a' by the bye,' he retorted. 'I'm here for another purpose at this time, to seek for my sister.'

He guessed that Sim was provoking him for that slight received on Helen's account but their encounter nearly came to blows again when Sim answered, deliberately insulting: 'Such wanton flesh is no worth the seeking.'

Johnny had raised his hand in fury to strike Sim in the face (and felt, piercingly, the pain of newly-mended muscles in his shoulder) when Sim's father came quickly between them as the raised voices and movement attracted general attention.

'They were wed before they went,' he said loudly, and then, sharply, over his shoulder to Sim: 'Leave your lies an' your mischief-making.' But Sim was well-content with the reaction he had provoked in Johnny and moved away silently, with a malicious smile on his face.

Johnny spoke urgently to Henderson: 'Will ye tell me the truth about my sister? I must know. It touches my honour nearly.'

The older man nodded. He led Johnny aside from the press of men and they stood alone by the great stone fireplace as Johnny had stood with his mother the previous night—so long ago, it seemed. This was the only place in those crowded halls where men and women drew away to let the head of the household speak privately with one of his family or with a guest.

'Ye'll have heard of Sander?' asked Henderson.

'Just,' said Johnny. 'Young Wat spoke o' him. The cousin that ye spoke of? An' was he the man who one o' my household saw wi' Helen?'

'It may be so,' said Henderson. 'It seems he brought her back on his saddlebow an'—she was no unwilling, Armstrong. She was no loose girl, I saw that for myself when I returned next day, but she and Sander had eyes for none but each other. It was strange.'

He mused a little, the firelight bright on his high-coloured face as the sunset had been, earlier. Johnny had always been told that he was a hard man, yet he had shown more feeling in this matter and seemed gentler than Johnny had ever expected. This surprised him; and he thought: why should men be enemies without knowing each other? Hugh had always sought to instil such hatred into Johnny, despite his mother's tolerance, and yet now Johnny could not find it in his heart to hate this rough, kindly man, for all he was his father's killer. That old quarrel and its outcome had been fair enough by all accounts save Hugh's, and it was long ago.

Henderson came to himself with a start. 'A very distant cousin of my boys, Alexander,' he said. 'He is a Douglas. From north and west o' here. A woman o' our family married up there in time past. An' they're an even more mixed breed than us Borderers. They've intermarried too, wi' the mountainy folk. They're Scots, when it comes to it. But his father and I kenned each other well enow in our youth, we were fostered together at a kinsman's north o' the Border. He went to take his place wi' his clan when his father died an' I've seen little o' him since. But he was travelling to Carlisle on business a while ago an' brought Sander here to stay. He an' my middle boys planned this mad jaunt. I said to send the girl back.'

He looked at Johnny with apology, surprising as it seemed, in his eyes.

'Some o' that I ken,' said Johnny impatiently. 'Where is she gone? Ye said they were wed?'

'Aye,' said Henderson. 'In the little chapel here when Douglas returned. He an' Sander would hae it so an' I, too, thought it best. As to where she is now, I canna tell ye. At home wi' the lad in all probability. I can only say north and west o' here. I dinna ken the place.'

Johnny said slowly: 'An old beggar brought me a message a while since that he said he had from a minstrel at your hall here. It seemed to be a message from Helen. The minstrel would ken where he got it an' could direct me. Can any here remember the lad?'

Henderson said: 'Robbie may ken, my eldest lad. He's wed, an' his head's straighter on his shoulders than the others'. What was the message, lad, an' the minstrel like?'

Johnny told him what he had heard from the old beggar. Henderson looked at him doubtfully.

'If 'tis true,' he said, 'should ye no leave well alone, lad?'

'I must know if 'tis true,' said Johnny violently.

Henderson nodded heavily. 'We'll ask Robbie.'

Johnny found himself grateful—another unexpected emotion.

Robbie was a big young man, chestnut-haired and ruddy-faced like his father, very conscious of his younger brothers' wildness, kindly, and responsible for much of the work of the farm.

He listened carefully to Johnny's description of the old beggar himself and then to the old man's description of the minstrel who had given him the message.

While Robbie stood musing, Johnny looked about him. He suddenly understood more of the implication of that phrase the beggar had used of the young minstrel: 'like a flame'. It had sounded so incongruous that Johnny had thought it no more than a description of the minstrel's professional costume. Now, himself coming in from the chill spring evening (even though more warmly clad than the old man had been), he saw that fire was the only brightness and warmth in such poor men's lives—and that therefore the minstrel must have been something special, apart from his gay costume. For the first time, he felt some curiosity as to the boy himself, quite apart from his role as messenger. What had it been about the minstrel that he should be remembered thus?

Robbie's face suddenly lit up and he smacked his clenched fist into his other palm. 'I mind me,' he said. 'How could I hae forgotten? The boy had a Southron-sounding name. Rainault? Aye, Rainault. Yon was the name. He was here in the winter. A good-looking, dark boy. Men said he was scenting up an' down the Border lands in search of some man on whom he wanted vengeance for a wrong. I dinna ken where he came from nor where he went from here, though it may hae been north-east. I am sorry.'

He also looked at Johnny with apology in his wide face. Johnny thanked him but his search seemed as far adrift as ever. What Robbie had told him *might* be of help; he might find this minstrel, and get the information he wanted from him. Then, again, the message might have come by other means before it reached the minstrel and Johnny would be none the wiser if he found him. Also, if Helen were in the west and he were to go east in his search, he moved further from her.

He could not decide on his next move.

Then Henderson spoke again. He understood Johnny's feelings well enough and would have felt the same in like circumstances, he admitted to himself. He was not over-concerned about Johnny's notions of honour but he had liked the little maid and thought her honour would do well enough.

Nevertheless he said: 'Ye'll need to find this minstrel, Armstrong. I canna send ye into the wilds, into Douglas country, as any messenger o' mine. Even wi' my word, I doubt ye'd get through. No man would take ye for a Henderson! It's in my mind that ye'll hae to pocket your pride.' He laughed and Johnny looked at him questioningly. 'Ye maun go among that kind, boy, an' follow the tide wi'out too many questions. An' ye canna go in those clothes for ye'll learn nothing. Disguise is the answer, an' real dirt. Ye maun beg like them whose confidence ye want.'

Again he laughed, though not maliciously. Johnny saw that he was right. No fastidiousness, nor vanity, had prevented his doing this before, only pride. For the first time, he grinned.

'Ye're maybe right,' he said, 'though I'll no relish the doing it.'

'Maybe no,' said Henderson, 'but 'tis the only way. An' no too many questions. Folk don't trust beggars who ask questions. Learn by indirection, Armstrong.'

The thought of such freedom excited Johnny strangely. Even the quest for Helen was obscured for the moment, by the prospect of journeying to this untravelled yet foot-loose boy.

Then Henderson said: ' 'Tis a wild goose chase, boy. Ye'll hae thought o' the difficulties yourself, no doubt. If ye find this minstrel, the message may hae come from another.' Johnny nodded. 'But if ye get no lead, ye can set off north-west on a chance. Ye'll maybe find her that way. It's no like our fells and dales, I've heard, but heather an' uplands an' bogs. Ye'll be a stranger there.'

Again Johnny nodded, grateful for the warning but not unwilling to venture into strangeness. Henderson looked at him shrewdly, a faint smile on his face. 'Is it your sister ye're seeking, Armstrong, or adventure?'

c

Johnny flushed. 'Helen first,' he said, 'o' course, Helen first. But I've no been far afield before.' He suddenly remembered his mother's parting words, saw their truth for him and glimpsed their bitterness for her. The astonishment of that moment repeated itself, with more understanding.

Henderson was laughing outright now. 'Ye'll do, boy,' he said. 'I thought ye something o' a dandy fellow at first but ye've fire in your belly right enough. Ye needed it to come over here, I surmise. I'll be sending those cattle o' yours back to your mother. Were any men killed in that skirmish?'

Johnny said, surprised: 'One. Hugh. An old companion o' my father's.'

Henderson frowned. 'I recall him. A good fighting man. I'll send your mother money for him.'

Johnny said: 'I wouldna hae asked that. He was living on our charity.'

'Your mother could use the money,' said Henderson sharply, his conscience perhaps pricking him. 'I'll send the full price for a fighting man.'

Johnny hesitated, then saw that all was fair and square now. 'My thanks,' he said. Then, awkwardly: 'There is no quarrel between us?'

'None,' said Henderson gladly. 'Nor ever was on my part. I only did what was required o' me those years ago. Nor would I carry enmity to an enemy's child. I'm no sorry to see an end to feuding an' raiding an' suchlike. My hand on it, Armstrong.'

So they clasped hands. Johnny saw that this was right, that he had indeed no quarrel with the man, that honour was satisfied in *this* matter, at least. Sim might mock as he pleased.

CHAPTER 6

The long search

I will drink o' the wan water
And eat o' the bread o' bran . . .

JOHNNY woke twice, briefly, during that night spent among the snoring men of the Henderson household— once to wonder at having made a friend of his enemy and at the surprising subtleties of a life that he had thought so simple, the second time to consider how he should set about getting clothes and disguise for his intended journey. Then he slept sound again till morning.

Henderson was away early the next day on some affair. He took Sim with him, probably deliberately, not wanting to leave potential trouble behind. Johnny was not sorry to see Sim go; he took the first opportunity he had to seek out Robbie. He had liked this eldest Henderson and was not too proud to ask his advice about his intended journey.

Robbie was in the yard, watching the cattle go out to pasture. The night had been frosty but the frost had soon moved under a bright sun and the yard was plashy under-foot as the herd moved out. Johnny glimpsed his own red heifer. Robbie laughed as he saw him glance at her. 'She'll be awa' to Banks in a day or two,' he said. 'My father said he'd send her. She'll go.'

Johnny gestured the remark away. He had no doubt that she would, nor that blood money would be paid for Hugh.

Robbie considered the question of the journey. He looked at Johnnie speculatively. 'Ye've too striking an appearance, Armstrong,' he said, 'to pass wi' just a change of clothes.' Johnny looked at him in surprise. He had no idea that his amber hair and vivid grey eyes made him a handsome figure; his looks were accentuated now by his grey clothes but even a change in these, as Robbie saw, would make little difference.

'But as to the clothes,' the Henderson went on, laughing, 'any o' my herdsmen'll change wi' ye gladly. Ask the lad yonder.' He indicated one of the ragged cheerful group of men behind the cattle. 'But leave your jacket wi' me, an' your horse an' sword. I'll see them safe till ye return.'

'If,' said Johnny briefly. Then: 'If no, will ye see that they get back to my brother?'

Robbie nodded. Such belongings were kept in the family. 'As to your looks, lad,' he said, 'ash in your hair an' rubbed into your face an' hands will age you admirably.' He had a nice turn of phrase. Johnny laughed. 'North-east, ye think?' he asked.

Robbie nodded. 'It's worth trying for a way,' he said.

Again Johnny was conscious of his own surprised gratitude and of acceptance of advice, from both Robbie and his father. He who had grown up believing that the rest of the world was his enemy, had found otherwise here, where most he might have expected enmity. Nor had he ever accepted advice at home; there I have a position to keep up, he told himself self-importantly. Then he had to admit ruefully that that self-importance was foolish and arrogant; also that he had no position here, that he was beholden to the Hendersons. And all this despite the feud that Hugh had still been urging on him with his dying breath! He saw that such a journey as he half-planned, half-knew to be inevitable, would require more acceptance of advice, and favours, and information. He must be suitably humble. He grimaced. Then the pleasurable excitement at the thought of his venture filled his mind again. It would be worth it.

During the morning he changed clothes with a Henderson herdsman about his age and size, who was delighted with his bargain; and Robbie spared time to superintend his change of identity and attempted disguise. Johnny felt himself different, and aged, in the very moment. His auburn hair became almost eerie in appearance under the grey dust of the ash; he screwed up his eyes as he rubbed ash into his face so that when he opened them again all the fine lines of an outdoor man's face, used to looking into distances, were more defined and accentuated.

Robbie looked at him critically. 'Ye look older,' he said, 'but no old. It's a young man's skin under that dirt. An' your eyes are young. Ye maun keep them downcast, boy —and pu' your sleeves over your hands. They're young, too, spite o' the dirt.'

Johnny thought a moment. 'I could limp,' he said. 'A young man aged by misfortune!' An unexpected touch of humour showed in him.

Robbie laughed. 'Ye could that,' he said. 'Good luck to ye.'

Johnny slipped out at the gate half an hour later, glad to be away before Sim returned. He remembered Hugh's dragging gait only too well and practised it up the hill eastwards. He had left his jacket and sword in Robbie's care but kept his dagger tucked in the belt around the dirty blue jerkin he wore; on that same belt he carried a shabby leather bag with scraps of food, a few groats, in it. He wore an old thick cloak, rent and ragged, that Robbie had found for him. Both of them suspected that these bits and pieces would never be handed back, that Johnny might never reclaim sword and jacket and horse.

*　　　*　　　*

For many weeks he roamed the Border lands, remembering to drag his right foot, renewing the ash in his hair in any quick moment of solitude at the edge of a fire. His face became naturally dirtier than ever, and browner, in the curious life of a beggar and in the strengthening sunlight of the growing year. He learned to pitch his voice low to disguise its strength, to be even more reticent than usual in the constant company of travellers. He offered nothing for the hospitality he received, neither song nor music nor juggling, simply the opportunity to men to improve their souls by giving. And, taking him for a young man aged and soured by the misfortune of his disablement, men gave him food generously, and the shelter of the shadowy ends of their halls, with a glimpse of flames on colder nights. He understood the old beggar's description of the minstrel well enough now. He asked quietly after that same minstrel wherever he went, and among the roving company that he kept, also. Sometimes men shook their heads; sometimes, their eyes brightening, they said that he had been there—how long before they were never quite certain although he was obviously vivid in their memories still—but was gone on, in which direction they did not know. These crumbs of possible proximity were sufficient to keep his search alive and alert.

He learned to accept charity with a good grace. Strange surroundings he welcomed. He found it difficult at first not to look around with a young man's interest at every new place he came to but quickly adopted the itinerant's habit of taking in much in swift, lowered glances that attracted no attention.

He had begun his long search by following the little river that flowed out of the moors through his and Henderson's land. Before he reached its actual head-waters, he had struck out through the mosses and bogs of the Bewcastle Waste on to the rough-grassed ridge of high land that was the source and watershed of the great rivers of the North—Tyne, Rede, Coquet, to the east and, to the west, Liddel Water, Teviot, Esk, and Tweed. In the valleys to the east, he heard mention of Rainault only at their heads, as if the minstrel had soon abandoned his search here and turned back to try the next valley.

Johnny wondered what this other man was seeking.

In the intervals between his enquiries after Rainault, Johnny found himself exhilarated by his own travelling. He did not even miss his horse as he had thought he might, having been accustomed to a mount for so many years that it had become an almost natural extension of himself. The company of others irked him a little but was often inescapable. When he did get the chance to travel alone, he took it with delight, forgetting his limp, lifting his head and his eyes to the wind and the hills and skies about him. He had never noticed them thus before. The tracks he walked were dusty and stony; he did not mind the discomfort. He looked with delighted surprise at the wider, richer valleys of the greater rivers and at the rounded, more luscious hills that enclosed them. Then he came to a settlement, or saw in the distance another party of vagrants, and he lowered his eyes, and shuffled again.

Poor men gave him shelter as well as the lords and yeomen of the greater houses. It was in the home of one such (a hut thick with smoke, on a foundation of cobblestones only, and with but branches and bracken for a roof, for poor men dared not yet build permanently after the years of devastation), set on the higher slopes at the head of Tynedale, in wild country in which he felt at home, that he came the closest to the mysterious Rainault that he had yet come.

He had returned to these fells after searching the more eastern valleys. It was June now, the elders and upland hawthorns in blossom, larks springing up from the heather before his feet as he climbed to the hills. In the valley below men had been busy at haymaking and sheep-shearing and he had thought, swiftly and shortly, of how they must be faring at Banks. In the longer days and the lighter evenings, he felt more hopeful of his quest, but was tired and hungry and was glad of the children calling to him to come in, by the hut, and of their mother's welcome at the low door. The interior seemed dark after the brightness outside and a small fire burned on the hearth in the centre, for cooking, as well as warmth on the chillier upland nights.

The family were kind; they offered Johnny a bowl of thick broth for the evening meal and he felt guilty at taking even that, seeing that this they all shared, seeing how much poorer was this home than his own. He accepted with gratitude, though, knowing that it would give offence if he did not do so, and being hungry. He asked after the minstrel, more out of habit than in expectation of a reply, but was astonished to find that this family remembered him particularly well and that he seemed not to be far ahead of Johnny, at last. They remembered him because he had not been too proud, for all his finery (or so the children thought it), to stay in the poor isolated hut, because he had paid for his lodging, because he had sung them songs.

The children's eyes lit up as they talked about him. Their mother said, gently: 'He was kind to the bairns and little more than a bairn himself. It canna be many nights since he was here. Dark? Sounding as if he came from a foreign land?'

'So I heard,' said Johnny. The woman looked at him sharply, her eyes keener on him than ever the eyes of servants in hall or tower, or even of his fellow-travellers, had been. He knew that she saw through his beggary. But men and women still did not ask too many questions of strangers along the Border. She gave him a quick smile and he smiled back—an easy, young man's smile, she saw that.

But she did ask, doubtfully: 'Ye mean him no mischief?' She too, obviously, had been fond of the dark traveller.

'None,' Johnny assured her. 'I seek his help.'

'Well then,' she said, 'I dinna ken the which way he came. My man brought him in. But he turned to the north-west when he left in the morning. I watched him go. Along the tops, maybe heading for Teviotdale. Only a while since.'

Johnny thanked her. He would not be sorry to turn west again himself; there was a haze on the sunniest days on these hills near the east coast that was unfamiliar to him, and unhomely.

He lay awake a long while that night in the hut, in the low light of the half-smothered embers of the fire, thinking more clearly of Helen than he had thought of her since he left home. Because the truth about her suddenly seemed nearer, he remembered her distinctly, no longer only an excuse for travelling but the thin shining girl who had so often teased his seriousness. And he wondered also, not for the first time, what this Rainault was like, whom people remembered well when they had seen him, who was 'like a flame'.

* * *

For all his feeling that he was nearer now to finding both Rainault and Helen, he despaired in the next few days of travelling, for he heard nothing of the minstrel and thought that he had lost the scent. He doubled back on his tracks through Teviotdale, to where he had first come down from the heather uplands after the night in the warm smoky hut, and began to work his way down the valley again, zigzagging from tower and fortified manor one side of the river to others on the further bank, in case he had just missed one small memory of the young man which would give him a further glimmer of hope. He travelled by himself, faster now so that he should not stay too long or too often under men's roofs and so make himself conspicuous. He slept under the stars some nights to avoid questions. He remembered his limp at times though it did not trouble him (on his own like this) as companions of the past had thought, sympathetically, that it must. He even felt a small pang of conscience at all that sympathy wasted on him; men, and women, had been kinder than he had ever thought they would be. Johnny Armstrong's knowledge of men was widening, his intolerance becoming more enlightened. He even noticed with pleasure that the farmers of Teviotdale were daring to grow crops; he had not known those parts in the days when no man dared sow grain for fear of the harvest lost before it could be gathered, but he guessed how it had been.

But still he heard nothing of Rainault. 'She wouldna hae lied to me,' he thought, of the woman at the hut. 'But maybe he took another track after he left there. If only I knew whom he was seeking I would better know where to look for him. Oh, must I go back again an' try other ways?' He was in despair. He felt that his search was as hopeless as ever.

Finally he decided to give up the quest for Rainault and set off for the Douglas lands on chance. He turned back to the head of Teviotdale and up on to the tops again; then he went down into the western valley of Eskdale—it led south at first but would at last direct his steps ever further west. He avoided the valley of Liddesdale where still no man *chose* to go.

He came one evening to a stronghold half-way down

Eskdale, on his way west, in mid-July. In the glimmering twilight he joined other vagrants waiting at the gate and went with them into the great hall where homeless men already sat among the shadows. He was in a black mood and went, by himself, to sit silently beside the stone steps leading to the upper floors where the family dwelt. He did not even hear at first the voice of a servant calling down from the upper floor: 'Rainault! Rainault the Frenchman! Are you there? My mistress wants music!'

Then the words registered on his mind. He looked up quickly, saw a dark boy, in shabby red and yellow minstrel's finery, rise in the shadows and detach himself from the dark company. He slung a lute over one shoulder and walked towards the foot of the steps by which Johnny had been sitting.

Johnny was up in a flash, moving forward to intercept the minstrel. He suddenly remembered his pretended limp and, in trying to adjust his gait accordingly, almost fell. The minstrel put out an arm laughingly. 'Hold up,' he said, and was about to add 'father', his hand on Johnny's arm, when he realised, from a glimpse of those vivid grey eyes in the gloom and the strength of the arm under his hand, that this was no old man that he was offering to help. He changed the address to *'mon ami'*.

Johnny straightened. 'I must speak with ye,' he said. 'I hae been seeking ye all the summer.'

The dark boy's eyes widened with amazement.

'Mais pourquoi?' he exclaimed, instinctively, in his native tongue. Then: 'I must go to the upper hall now. The lady wants me. We will speak together as soon as I may come down.'

His English was good but clipped, a foreigner's English. He was almost as tall as Johnny but slighter, so that he seemed younger; also his skin was as smooth and golden as a child's still. But because he was dark, his first faint beard showed as a fine shadow on his upper lip and along his jawline and gave him a sophisticated air. Yet his smile was very sweet.

Johnny drew back as the minstrel went up the steps in answer to another impatient call.

CHAPTER 7

The minstrel

The youngster was clothed in scarlet red,
In scarlet fine and gay . . .

RAINAULT'S voice was fine and light; Johnny heard his
singing from the floor above, with the sweet lute accom-
paniment, as he leaned against the wall in long waiting.
The singing surprised and fascinated him. He had heard
nothing like it before. Hugh had used to growl out old
songs of the Border quite often and he had heard pipes
and fiddle and drum occasionally at Brampton market but
never anything like this gentle and melancholy music.

When the minstrel eventually came down the stairs,
Johnny involuntarily asked him first what he had been
singing, forgetting for the moment all the questions he had
been waiting so long to ask. Rainault laughed: 'Foolish
songs, *mon ami*. Not suited to this country but the lords
and ladies like to hear them. Of love. It is fashionable.'

He laughed again but Johnny thought that he heard
bitterness behind the equally fashionable laziness of the
young voice.

'They sounded sad,' he said. This, again, was not what
he had intended to say at all but it followed naturally
from the songs and the dark boy's disillusioned speech and
laugh.

'It *is* sad,' said Rainault, and this time there was no
mistaking the bitterness in his voice. He shrugged. 'Why
have you been seeking me?' he asked gently.

Johnny returned to the moment abruptly. 'In the

spring I had a message from an old beggar,' he said, wondering how to explain what seemed a complicated tale. 'I learned at last that it seemed that ye had given it him, from my sister. She was carried off to Scotland in the winter. Is this so?'

Some perplexity remained in the minstrel's face. 'I've no explained well,' said Johnny, 'and may be, after all, ye are no the man I sought.'

But then the dark boy's beautiful golden face cleared. 'You are Johnny Armstrong of Banks,' he exclaimed delightedly. 'Your sister Helen?'

Johnny nodded hurriedly. 'Did she herself give ye the message?' he asked urgently. 'Where is she? Can ye tell me the way?'

Rainault lifted his hands, laughing. 'One question at a time,' he said. 'It was many months ago. But, yes, she gave me the message herself. And the place I found by mistake, I was misdirected by mischievous men. Can I tell you how to get there? I do not know. I can show you part of the way. Will that serve?'

Johnny nodded vigorously. 'My thanks,' he said. 'I hae more questions to ask ye. May I? But hae ye not business o' your own?'

Again Rainault's face clouded. 'Yes,' he said, 'and it is with an Armstrong. Not you, *mon ami*.'

'There are many o' us,' said Johnny. 'We're near one o' the Armstrong strongholds here, up in Liddesdale.'

'I know,' said Rainault. Then he was silent.

'Who is it that ye seek?' asked Johnny gently. Instant liking for this boy had sprung up as they first spoke and the impatience and short temper natural to Johnny were quietened by the minstrel's own gentleness; though keeping his temper under control was something that Johnny had also been learning from his way of life since the spring.

Rainault sighed. 'I have told no one yet,' he said.

'Maybe I am afraid to find him.' He smiled rather wanly. But he was as attracted to Johnny as the Armstrong was to him. An easy and true familiarity, not usual with either of them, had developed almost immediately they had met. Both were surprised. Rainault said—on impulse, but he knew it to be true: 'I will perhaps tell *you*. But now we will sit and eat and you shall ask me your questions.'

Rainault had food in his wallet. He shared it with Johnny, both sitting companionably with their backs against the side of the stone steps. As the great fire in the hall flamed up—for it was always cold in these thick-walled towers—they felt warmed by more than the flames and light, and the intimacy of their first conversation increased.

'You are no beggar,' said Rainault, 'and your limp is false, *mon ami*.'

Johnny took no offence, the minstrel's voice was sweet and teasing. 'It is so manifest?' he asked.

'Perhaps only to myself,' smiled Rainault. 'You were so impatient to speak with me!'

Johnny grinned. 'I had given up hope of finding ye,' he said. 'Ye went down into the dales and came back and crossed your ain path and recrossed it—I didna ken where ye nor I were going!'

'You have been tenacious,' said the other boy. 'What can I tell you?'

'Of Helen,' said Johnny. 'Where did ye see her?'

'It was in the cold,' said Rainault, sighing gustily, 'but since Christmas. I was a fool to travel these lands in winter. But men in Carlisle sent me up there, north and west, into Nithsdale, and men of her husband's family found me and brought me in. You know she is wed?'

Johnny nodded.

'She was kind to me,' said Rainault. 'She asked my story. I told her more than I have told any. She learned that I was coming east again—I had discovered that there were no Armstrongs in those lands—and she asked me to get that message to you. It should have kept you home, Johnny!'

'I'm bound to see for myself,' muttered Johnny.

'She was happy,' said Rainault, 'she and her golden husband.'

'He snatched her from us,' said Johnny, angry again at the memory. 'My honour is at stake unless I know she went willingly. An' she must tell me so herself. I am head o' my family.'

Rainault shrugged and spread his hands. '*I* tell you, *mon ami*,' he said, 'that she is happy, that she must have been willing. Has it hurt your pride so, Johnny Armstrong o' Banks?'

Johnny growled at him, then saw his smile, softened, and wondered whether what Rainault suggested was the truth after all.

'You will still go, I see,' said Rainault. 'I will show you what I can. It was rough and dirty then, their life in the winter and snow. But I remember something of how I returned. Her husband is a Douglas, *n'est-ce-pas*?'

Johnny understood the tone if not the language.

He nodded. He said reluctantly: 'I shall no disturb her if I see all is well.'

'You have come a long way for this,' said Rainault. 'Round and about. I know your home. I knew there were Armstrongs there but I also knew that they were not those I sought.'

'Tell me,' said Johnny, forgetting his own troubles. 'Who and why?'

'Not here,' said Rainault, looking round. 'Not among others. It haunts me.'

Johnny was silent.

Then, to relieve the tension, he asked: 'What's a Frenchman doing on the Border anyway?'

But Rainault refused to be drawn even that far yet, although he knew that Johnny's question was unintentionally curious, and more teasing than inquiring. He retorted: 'What's an Armstrong doing in beggar's clothes?'

Johnny was seriously indignant. 'I'd no get far in my proper gear,' he said. 'Armstrongs are no very popular in these parts. And I canna wear popinjay clothes like yours for disguise. *I've* no singing voice to charm the ladies!'

His voice was roughly teasing again by the end of his speech; such lightness was not usual with him. The liking behind it was clear.

Rainault lifted a hand. 'A fair hit,' he said, laughing, 'but I would like to see you as you really are, Johnny.'

Then he teased in return. 'Was there not another Johnny Armstrong once? I seem to have heard tales and a crude song or two about him.'

'There hae been Johnnys, Jocks, an' Jacks, all Armstrongs,' said Johnny. 'The one ye ken lived some years ago, they've made songs on him. He was a Liddesdale Armstrong. Do ye no think your man may live in these parts?'

'It is possible,' said Rainault, without enthusiasm. 'I will see you on your way tomorrow before I think of that.'

So they sat on quietly, in very friendly fashion. During the evening, the gentry came into the main hall and Rainault was called to sing again. The lonely-sounding music, the foreign words, haunted Johnny; but he did not ask about them again when Rainault returned to his place for he remembered the tone of the answer last time he had asked.

When the torches were doused for the night, the two young men, contrasting so strikingly in colouring and clothes, rolled themselves in their cloaks and laid themselves down at the side of those steps where they had met each other.

D

CHAPTER 8

By Solway Sands

... And she did sigh and say 'Alas!
That ever I loved a man!'

WHEN the two set off next morning, the day was sunny
and the sky cloudless. They travelled alone, keeping a
distance between themselves and a group of beggars in
front of them. The river flashed and tumbled as Johnny
remembered his own little river was used to do. The hills
beyond were not so very different from his own smooth,
rounded fells. Alder trees grew along the banks of the Esk.
There seemed no evil in men or nature. Yet this valley,
and the valley of Liddel Water that ran into it from the
north, and the wide moss at the head of the Solway Firth
that they would come to soon, were thick with the sites
of battle and foray, burning and plundering, not so
many years before, and with songs of those same battles.
Johnny knew something of all these things but not in any
order. They were the tales of his childhood and boyhood,
little more. But he indicated Liddesdale as they saw its
mouth in the distance, quiet and green this morning as if
violence had never issued from it; he recognised it from
stories he had been told, from talk he had heard in recent
days.

All the alders along the banks of the Liddel Water had
been chopped down. They might have provided cover for
any unwise invaders of the dale. Rainault shuddered as
he gazed at it when Johnny told him what it was.

'A dark place,' he said. 'Dark despite the sunlight.'

Johnny looked at him curiously. 'What do ye ken o' it?' he asked. ' 'Tis more peaceable these days, I've heard.'

'Only tales and songs,' said Rainault. 'There is a dark sensation about it though.'

Johnny was impressed and rather moved by the expression on the minstrel's face. He had heard of the look of doom that men sometimes wore. This seemed it.

He laughed the feeling away. 'Did ye no come through it as ye came back from seeing Helen?' he asked. ' 'Tis the shortest way up on to the tops.'

Rainault shook his head. 'Nay,' he said. 'I came to the mouth of this river Esk and there is another valley runs up to the—Bewcastle Waste, I think it is called?' Johnny nodded. 'Then down to the Henderson fort.'

'Aye,' said Johnny. 'An easier way. But if ye seek Armstrongs, there's the place.'

'Yes,' said Rainault, 'I have avoided them, have I not? Even you.' His smile was bitter.

Johnny was silent for a while; then he said: 'I'll back ye, if ye want help. When I hae seen Helen.'

Rainault turned to him impulsively. 'Johnny, you are generous,' he said. 'Indeed, I am no fighter.' He spread his sensitive fingers wide, expressively. 'In my first fury, I thought to take vengeance hot and bloodily. It has cooled a little since then, and my courage also. It must be attempted though.'

Johnny asked no more questions. 'I will tell you soon,' said Rainault.

The two walked on steadily down the valley.

'You are forgetting your limp, Johnny,' observed Rainault suddenly, light-hearted again.

'Pretence is no necessary wi' ye,' said Johnny. Then, grinning: 'Some days 'tis no so bad as others.'

Any from Banks would not have believed the apparently humourless Johnny capable of such a joke, so seriously had he always taken himself and his position as head of the household; but Rainault's joyousness, combined with a sense of escape from responsibility, had released a latent spring of mischief, however grim, in the sober Armstrong.

Rainault laughed full-throatedly. 'You are not so grave as you appear, Johnny,' he said. 'But it is only the limp that makes you appear a beggar. You stand like a free man at other times.'

'Do I so?' said Johnny, in some surprise.

'We are both shabby enough, though,' said Rainault, looking down ruefully at his own gay-seeming apparel that was yet worn to the grain, 'for beggars. You do not need your limp, Johnny.'

'I needs must keep it,' said Johnny. 'Why else would a young man beg the roads unless he were no able-bodied?'

Rainault considered, and nodded. '*Vraiment*,' he said; then laughingly translated for Johnny's puzzled benefit: 'Truly. Indeed. It is so.'

'Where did ye learn your English?' Johnny asked.

'At courts,' said Rainault. 'At courts and petty capitals.' He grimaced. 'One needs two tongues at least to be a minstrel.' There was the note of disillusion in his voice that Johnny had heard before, and again the Borderer wondered at the sweetness that had survived so obviously bitter an upbringing.

They looked about them with interest as they went, Johnny because this land was all strange to him, Rainault —although the land here was strange to him also—because he, too, was of the roving kind. The same curiosity in them both drew them close, as well as the mutual bond of the message and journey.

Johnny glanced up and saw the clear blue of the sky beginning to streak with fine feathers of high white cloud and a mottling in the south-west. 'Rain to come,' he said briefly.

Rainault groaned. 'It is the worst weather for wanderers,' he said. 'How can you tell, Johnny?'

Johnny nodded upward. 'I ken our skies too well,' he said.

By noon they had left behind the small hills of Eskdale and come to the flat ditched land of the great Solway Moss. This was doubly strange to Johnny; he paused to admire the dykes and the rich pasture land between. Farming, for all he had been glad to leave it behind, was too much in his blood for him to fail to notice such advantages. He envied the men who farmed here for their easy living, though he remembered also that this had been the real Debatable Land of the recent past, and no wonder. He knew that there were Armstrongs hereabout also, but no details of them, and did not like to remark on their presence to Rainault who seemed gay and carefree for the moment, laughing at Johnny's awe of the good land.

He pointed to low hills and a valley to the east. 'Thus I went,' he said, 'along a side river that runs into this. It took me to the Bewcastle Waste—ah, in bad weather, Johnny, and the ground quaking!'

He looked at Johnny with horror. 'Mosses,' said Johnny, laughing. 'Bogs an' such. Wander into yon, lad, and there's an end o' ye.'

'So I guessed,' said Rainault. 'A wild land, Johnny.'

'I ken no other,' said Johnny. 'My own farm is no much fairer than the Waste.'

'You do not long for it again?' asked Rainault.

'Nay,' said Johnny, laughing. 'I farm but am no farmer. Travelling suits me fine.'

'Who is to care for the farm?' asked Rainault.

'My brother,' said Johnny, 'and my mother, I dare say. There are folks in plenty while I'm away.'

Rainault nodded.

During the afternoon they went through Annan, crossed the Annan Water by its little sturdy bridge, and came among the sand-dunes and on to the shore of the Solway Firth itself, just as the tide began to turn and the sun, to the south-west, glimmered on the smooth and filling water. Alone now on the long track that snaked east and west above the tide-line, and the sky curdling above them to milky cloud without a break, they stood to watch for a while. The tide came in soundlessly and fast over weed and pebbles and the narrow stretch of sand below the bank on which they stood: it had a power and speed about it which was eerie.

'Men are trapped half-over, I have heard,' said Rainault. 'It is alarming.'

'Ye'd need to ken its ways,' agreed Johnny.

They were bemused by the brimming water; they watched it as in a dream.

'I shall tell you,' said Rainault, as if half-asleep, then shook his head to speak more clearly. 'I know where we may seek shelter for the night, it is near, but there we may not speak easily alone. And so, and also because you have told me of yourself, I will tell you my story, Johnny, before this dreadful water.'

He squatted, taking up a handful of pebbles, and Johnny squatted beside him, not looking at him because a new-found care for others told him that Rainault would find the story hard to tell.

'I grew up in a court, a little French court,' said Rainault steadily, 'I and my sister. And she was waiting-maid to the daughter of the court, and I soon minstrel. My fingers were on the strings of harp and lute for as long as I may remember. The daughter wed an Englishman—he came to the court often, he had fought for my lord at some time, a paid soldier—a mercenary?' Johnny nodded. Rainault continued. 'And so Ambrosine went to England with her

mistress and sent me back word, by another minstrel, that
here was occupation, and money, if I grew tired of home.
And I did grow tired of home, very soon. Our mother was
dead. We were bastard-born, but of the same father—our
mother had assured us this—though he was dead also,
long ago. Indeed, we loved each other well. It was in York
that I found her when I came to England—no colder
than Britanny, *mon ami!*—but then the lord and lady
moved on, to Carlisle. My lord was to be a Warden of
this Border?' Again Johnny nodded. 'So,' said Rainault,
satisfied with his recital thus far. 'That great red castle,
that was cold. But my lady kept my sister well, and
I, too, grew fine!' He laughed without bitterness, remembering good days. 'But in that castle and in that
town mixed men of many sorts, with suits to my lord,
of both sides of the Border—I could not understand it
all—and there was one Will Armstrong come to plead
a cause.'

His voice became hard. He tossed the pebbles into the
grey tide that almost brimmed the bank. 'Men called him
Ill Will. I saw no reason—then. A big man, some ten
years older than my sister, handsome, of good carriage.
She was an easy prey for him, who thought herself so
proud and worthy of a marriage portion. *Ma pauvre!* He
got her with child and was away again, back to his hills,
satisfied in his cause and satisfied in his lust and finished
with her. So. She loved him greatly. There is no accounting
for love. She went one day to one of the towers and threw
herself from there and when they told me and I came, she
was dead and broken, and the babe within her. She de-
served better than that, with her beauty, and her care for
me. Our causes are something alike, Johnny. I, too, come
for vengeance but I am faint-heart, I think. But your man
has wed your sister. Why do you seek him out then? It is
not *necessaire*. It is my sister's unhappiness I seek to

avenge, no loss of honour, as you people call it. But *your* sister is happy. What *is* this honour the Border speaks of?'

He stood up, expecting no answer. Johnny stood up beside him, silently.

'We are both far from home,' said Rainault, 'if we have a home, we wandering men. And you will pursue your man, and I, maybe, mine, and little will come of either chase.'

The tide was now full, the sky greying, and, as they turned west again, they felt the coming drizzle on their faces. Rainault unslung his lute from his shoulder. He brought out a folded bag of leather from his pouch, opened it wide, and drew it over the precious instrument lest the damp should harm its strings.

'So,' he said, tying the laces of the lute-cover slowly, and answering one of Johnny's first questions of him the night before, 'that is what a Frenchman does on the Border.'

'Aye,' said Johnny. 'I am sorry.' He spoke quietly, and meant it.

'But not very successfully,' said Rainault wryly. There was shame in his voice too.

'I'll back ye,' said Johnny. 'I hae given ye my word I would.'

Rainault looked at him through the growing dusk and the fine rain.

'Am I a coward, Johnny?' he asked.

'I'd no think that,' said Johnny, looking back at him steadily. 'Ye left an easy life. An' men's sisters hae been debauched and deserted before an' no vengeance sought. Ye'd no need to tramp the roads.'

'She killed herself,' said Rainault. '*En effet*, he was her murderer.'

'Aye,' said Johnny heavily. 'But I wouldna think ye

coward, just a mite out o' place. Wait ye, Rainault, we'll go together. He doesna deserve to escape.'

This was the first time that Johnny had used Rainault's name; the Breton was warmed by the word and the manner of its use.

They went on, into the now heavy rain.

CHAPTER 9

Nithsdale

. . . For so that I your company
May have, I ask no more.

Two days more of travelling brought them to Dumfries, on the river Nith, which flowed south. This was the largest town that Johnny had ever seen, a place of wonder after the small irregular grey market-place in the valley below Banks, which was all his previous experience of marts. Rainault laughed at him softly as they went about the grey streets together and Johnny looked with amazement at the many open-fronted shops, and the cobbled squares, and the fine horsemen who spurred about in the crowded streets.

'This is nothing, *mon ami*,' said Rainault, 'compared with Carlisle, with York, with London!'

Johnny laughed. He felt something of the excitement that men experience in towns—the sense of novelty, of being among many of their kind, of living where events take place—but he was not comfortable with walls around him.

'I'm no so struck as I seem!' he said. 'Towns are no for me, in truth. I'm easier in the fells.'

'So,' said Rainault. 'We must go on, in any case, while your short summer holds. I remember some of the way up Nithsdale but it was there that I was lost in snowdrifts'— he shuddered—'and the Douglas men found me. Therefore I cannot give you full directions to the fort, being bemused by snow, both coming and going!'

'A little will serve,' said Johnny. 'I've a tongue in my head—though folk may no be too ready to tell me o' the place. But I am become more used to finding out, this summer.'

So, after a night in the castle hall, when Rainault was called on to sing and was in great favour, so that Johnny scowled at the fine folk who might take friend and guide from him—though Rainault was deaf to any flattery or requests that might divert him from his way—they set out from the poor edges of the town on the stony track that led north up the dale.

Since that rainy evening by the Solway Firth, the weather had remained grey and comfortless. It was cold journeying, but dry now at least, and, as they went, keeping themselves solitary, the fells loomed about them again and Johnny felt more at ease and Rainault glad for him. The Borderer had not renewed his disguise since they left Dumfries, knowing that in this wild land he was barely noticed beside the unaccustomed presence and gallant if grimy colours of the minstrel; his grey eyes were young and vivid in his tanned face and something of the underlying amber glowed in his tangled hair.

Rainault looked at him admiringly. 'Johnny, you are beautiful!' he said.

Johnny stared in absolute astonishment, then laughed until he almost choked.

'Nay,' said Rainault, laughing too, 'it is the truth, *mon ami*. You would make a courtier by your looks.'

Johnny had recovered but was still grinning. 'I'm no smooth enow for courts and halls,' he said.

'No,' agreed Rainault, 'you are not smooth—though you are more tender than you think—but I would wish to see you in good clothes.'

Johnny thought of his grey Lodden and his quilted jacket back beyond the Wall. He shrugged. 'These are good enow for the time,' he said. 'Rags best serve a wanderer.'

'And you are enjoying a wandering life,' smiled Rainault.

'Aye,' said Johnny. 'Aye, I am. Why so?'

'You have the wanderlust,' said Rainault, 'as I have also. We like to see the world.'

Johnny laughed. 'I've no come far,' he said.

'It will serve,' said Rainault, 'for now.'

Nithsdale was lonelier than most of the dales that they had come through, separately or together; the character of the soil was diffcrent so that here grew ferns and gorse and heather, and the tracks were sandier. The heather was in flower and its colour beautiful to the two wandering boys.

Such land supported little farming. Surprisingly, however, Rainault noticed before Johnny did that in the lower stretches of the valley some of the moorland had been cleared, and farms, in the style of the richcr lands of the Border, had been planted. 'Small enough as yet,' said Rainault, remarking on this to Johnny, 'but the work will grow. And men will make more. They are stubborn, and many like a challenge.' He grinned ruefully.

Johnny looked at these neat, stone-walled pastures and low stone houses, set snugly in the landscape, with some admiration; but this was back-breaking farming and of little interest to him in any case.

The small farms fell away as they journeyed further north into more purple lands; the dwellers in these harsher reaches of the valley lived by herding and hunting only and were poor folk. They were more hospitable than their country though, kindly and generous, and always ready to welcome the two strangers for hospitality's sake alone.

Because the land was poor, there were no towns, nothing to draw beggars; so Johnny and Rainault travelled by themselves, slowly, both quite content in the moment,

astonishingly happy in each other's company. There was
no need of disguise, for none here looked at Johnny with
suspicion, nor thought to question his condition and pur-
suit, and so his true appearance now began to show even
more clearly through his rags. Johnny and Rainault were
both amazed to notice that, at the places off the track
where they stayed to eat or sleep (and Rainault always
paid, with a few groats from his scanty store), many of the
men had looks like Johnny's—tall, wide-shouldered, a sort
of silvered-auburn in their hair, the light and vivid eyes.

'Does your family come from these parts, Johnny?'
Rainault had asked when the likeness first became
obvious.

Johnny shook his head. 'Nay,' he said. 'Border born and
bred. But wait ye—my mother has such a look, though she
came from south and west o' the Wall. It is maybe the
look o' the west!' They were interested and amused.

The music that they heard startled them too. These were
musical people and always there was the simple fiddle,
the small bagpipes, in the evenings, or, among the hills,
the shepherd boys' pipes, to play tunes, that wandered,
returned, embroidered every phrase. This music had a
barbaric sound about it that made them wince at first—
Johnny used to the simple beat of the ballads, Rainault
to his own sweet melodies; and when Rainault played his
sophisticated music sometimes for the rough people who
gave them shelter, they were equally surprised. Rainault
set himself to learn some of this strange music and soon
found it as melancholy-sweet as that which he had played
since youth. Johnny was even sooner enthralled; it spoke
to him like a family voice.

The wind had changed as they journeyed slowly on. It
blew softly from the north-west, breaking the cloud, bring-
ing blue evenings that were colder and shorter but lovely
while they lasted. There was beginning to be a touch of

autumn in the air. The bracken was deepening in colour, they heard the stags belling in the hills.

One morning, Rainault walked more slowly and looked about him with uncertainty. 'I know no further, Johnny,' he said. 'Somewhere about here I must have become lost. The Douglas men took me up into the hills and I do not even know in which direction. I can be no more help to you.'

Johnny smiled at him. 'Dinna fret, lad,' he said. 'I'll find my ain way. Ye'll no come wi' me?'

Rainault shook his head. 'You will manage your business better without me, Johnny. I will back to Dumfries. I am a creature of towns, *mon ami*.'

'Aye?' said Johnny. 'But wait ye there till I return.'

They stopped on the track, facing each other. Rainault put his hands on Johnny's upper arms in what was almost an embrace. 'Take care of yourself, *mon ami*,' he said softly. 'Take care, Johnny.'

Johnny smiled, put his right hand up to touch Rainault's right hand swiftly. Such deliberate contact was rare for him.

'Wait for me,' he repeated.

And so they parted, each sad to see the other stepping away. Johnny, who had known no man well in all his life, was almost desolate at the loss of that boy—the boy 'like a flame'—known for so short a while and already loved. He had cared for no one thus before—save perhaps Helen, of whom he now thought as he turned north. Helen was part of the world of far-away home; something of the gentleness that had grown between himself and Rainault remained with him but the thought of Helen roused in him the Border starkness and hardness again. He thought: she must be found, questioned, perhaps retrieved. The family's honour must be saved; it mattered no less because he had now to wear rags in order to save it.

He renewed his disguise, rubbing his hands into the peaty soil that underlay banks of heather and then into his hair and over his face; he remembered to limp again.

He asked for the Douglas stronghold at the lonely huts he came upon and of shepherds whom he encountered when he left the track and went upon the hillsides. All those to whom he spoke directed him further north and west, without telling him the exact location. They were curious about this traveller, who sometimes limped and sometimes forgot to limp, as they observed with sharp eyes; but there seemed no harm in him so the word was passed round in swift, secret ways, that he was seeking the Douglas. And, one evening, as he stood on a hillside, looking for a patch of shelter where he might spend the night and feeling as far from his goal as ever, three young men, bright-haired and hard-eyed (for they only did their lord's bidding and had no care themselves for this vagrant) came upon him and spoke to him courteously, as was always their habit, caring or no. He did not understand their language but he heard the word 'Douglas' and went with them.

He lost all sense of direction as they took him by a deliberately roundabout way to the fort. Its earthen ramparts, when they came to them in the last of the dusk, seemed primitive to him, but the hall itself was well-built of timber, felled in the woods of small oak that grew about the lower hills. It was smokier than other halls he knew though, for the fire still burned on a central hearth here, as in older days, as in the peasant's hut above Tynedale, and the pungent smoke found its way out slowly through a hole in the roof. The people were hospitable; he was given a place by the fire, and broth and oatcakes. No questions were asked this evening when a traveller might be tired.

Presently, as the light dimmed further and spluttering heather torches were lit around the hall, to supplement

the firelight, the Douglas and his son took their places at
the high table, and the son's wife came in from the
women's quarters, carrying her baby son in her arms.

It was Helen. She was as slim as Johnny remembered
her but looking taller in a gown of dark green, with a long
scarf of chequer-patterned woollen in rich bright colours
over one shoulder and looped about her body; she carried
the babe proudly and only handed him to another woman
to be taken back to sleep when the clan had seen him and
acclaimed him.

Johnny, ducking his dusty head in the gloom beyond
the fire, was part-fascinated, part-horrified by this barbaric spectacle. Helen wore rough gold at her throat and
on her arms, and a circlet of gold with fine chains hanging
from it in her dark hair—it glistered in the smoky light.
She did not seem his sister. But Helen it was. He had never
seen before that she was beautiful. What strange world
was this that she lived in now? She looked a queen, a
woman, no girl any longer, and quite radiant with happiness. This was a far cry from Banks. Had he the right to
interfere?

Chapter 10

Kindred

. . . Then out and spake her brother dear:
'I bear the sword shall gar him die.'

His feelings had changed somewhat by the next morning.
As he woke, he was thinking furiously: Rainault did not
tell me she was with child! Then he woke fully and thought
clearly: he could not have noticed then, that early, in the
winter. The memory of Rainault brought a smile to his
lips. He had not been furious with Rainault in his dream,
but with Helen. He roused himself and sat up; the embers
of the fire were still glowing, fresh peat had been placed
round them, tousle-haired men were stirring all over the
hall in the greyness. The atmosphere of amber splendour
of the evening before was quite gone in the cool light of
dawn.

He sat up, reaching instinctively to touch his fingers
in the ash and dabble his hair with the soft warm dust of
it. After eating what was offered to him and thanking
the men who brought it, he watched the activities in the
hall. The women were crowding together, each taking a
soft basket of rushes under her arm—apparently there
were berries to be harvested from the hillsides and the day
was to be fine, so that the berries would soon be dry
enough to pick.

When the women trooped out, he followed them, at
some loss what to do next, how or even whether to try to
approach Helen in this unfamiliar world. He could see for
himself that she was happy. There was really no need to

E

do other than go quietly back down Nithsdale and find Rainault. But some strong impulse made him wish to speak with her, question her, even upbraid her for her happiness. He did not recognise this feeling as jealousy.

Still nobody had questioned him about his errand. All, with an instinctive courtesy, waited for him to make it known when he was ready. They had brought him to the Douglas homestead, as they had heard he wished; now, nobody pressed him. He was a guest. He would speak in his own good time.

He went out of the hall and sat in the early sunlight against the gate, brooding and beggarly. Helen came out, with a group of women, laughing. She held a basket under her outstretched left arm and her long plaid was wrapped across her shoulder and her back. Within its folds the babe lay sleeping soundly, warm against his mother's spine. An equal world indeed, where the chief's daughter-in-law went berry-picking with the other women and carried her child girdled against her. But no kindness came into Johnny's eyes as he looked up at her when she passed.

The women went up the hillside, in this last group, and then began to spread out, among the purpling of the heather and in the sunlight that now flooded the slopes. Each took her own path, making for patches of hillside where she knew the berries grew well, and began to gather them. But a communal song, the soft seasonal singing peculiar to this end-of-summer occupation, drifted down from the many throats towards the hall.

Johnny, looking after them as they went, saw Helen clearly in her warm-coloured gown and plaid and noticed that she was working her way across the hillside towards a hollow which she obviously knew well. She would not be visible from the fort there, nor, when she moved down into it, to any of the other women on the hill, for a short while at least.

Seeing this, Johnny suddenly made up his mind, got to his feet, and began to move slowly up the sandy path that the women had taken. Nobody seemed to notice him. All were busy. Summer was nearing its end and there was much to do.

Presently he branched off the track, through the heather, following Helen.

When he came upon her, in the warm, scented dip of ground, she was crooning to herself, or to the baby, as she bent to pick the firm dark berries. She suddenly sensed his approach and looked up and was startled to see the tall beggar making his way down towards her. She had noticed him, vaguely, the previous night, having heard of his apparent quest, but had only been sorry, momentarily, for the bowed figure beyond the fire, and thought no more of him. Now, however, she was a little alarmed, for he no longer stooped, nor limped, and there was an air of strength and purpose about his stride and his approach. His eyes were fixed on hers as he came.

Abruptly, she straightened, dropping her half-filled basket.

'Johnny!' she said. Neither his filthy clothes nor his dulled hair distracted her attention from those startling, familiar eyes, so grey, so bright. So cold, too, she saw with some misgiving.

'Aye,' he said. 'Johnny.'

He stood before her, taller than she. Even the lines round his mouth were familiar to her now.

'Did ye no get my message?' she asked.

'Aye, I got the message,' he said, his gaze still firmly on her.

'Then why did ye come?' she asked, haughtily now, her heart fluttering for this beloved brother but angry at the criticism that she felt in his tone and his looks.

'My honour needed answers,' he said, more roughly to

her high air. 'Did ye come o' your own free will? Or were ye forced? He had no right to take ye like that.'

'Answers ye shall have,' she answered proudly. 'I came willingly. I sent the message to put your mind at ease. Ye did wrong to ignore it. Your conceit of yourself and your honour is too great. It always was.'

His eyes flickered a little at this, her old unmistakeable way of stating home truths. But he would not be deterred from the course he had now set himself. He also was angry.

'But he took ye,' he said. 'Did ye no fight when he scooped ye to his saddle? Or were ye willing then, too?'

He saw her eyes soften with memory and was furious to be so excluded, his question unanswered. She remained silent, remembering complicated emotions not easily to be explained to an angry brother.

Then he said, nodding roughly at the child: 'By God, yon was quick doing.'

He meant to wound her. His accusing tone infuriated her also; it drove the softness that had so hurt him from her eyes.

'It is nigh a year,' she said, proudly and coldly, 'since I left Banks.'

Now Johnny was furious. '*Left?*' he stormed, '*left?* Then ye were no *taken?*'

Astonishingly, she laughed. 'Oh, some o' this,' she said, 'an' some o' that.' She was still laughing quietly.

He stared at her, completely taken aback by this sudden, unexpected change of attitude in her, by the sweet familiarity of her happy laugh.

She raised her right arm and gently swung the plaid with the sleeping babe in it round before her.

'Oh, Johnny,' she said, 'let us no be angry wi' each other. I am happy, ye can see that for yourself. An' look at the babe. Maybe he *was* got out of wedlock. What matters that? We were wed within weeks. An' he is the heir.'

She looked down passionately at the little sleeping face though the babe's lids were fluttering as he began to wake. He was fair, more ashen than Johnny, and his eyes, when he opened them now, were blue still but shading to a bright grey.

'He is like ye,' said Helen gently. 'His name is Ewen. It is the form for John up here. He is called after ye.' She had hesitated a little. So much she felt herself to be of this people, that she had nearly said: 'That is how we say John up here.' But she knew that that would have implied identification of herself with the Douglases and would have further angered her brother. Yet she did not speak of her husband's people as 'they'. Johnny noticed that, though he would have noticed 'we' even more quickly. As he looked at the child, still with hostility, it suddenly smiled at him, a smile toothless, delicate, completely engaging, with a general air of benison, and yet directed particularly at him.

He wrenched his gaze away, feeling his heart too stirred, his anger too softened.

Helen said quietly, sensing the sudden softness in her brother: 'He is your nephew, Johnny, he is your sister's son.'

The tie between a man and his sister's son was strong in both societies; Johnny glanced again at the child. He was unused to such small creatures but suddenly noticed the minute fingernails glimmering on the tiny clasped hands; it smiled at him once more.

He said, quietly: 'God's blessing on the bairn.'

Helen sighed. 'Ye'll no understand, Johnny. How could ye? Ye've no felt it yet! but we *couldna* part. He took me up an' I let him, an' when we were back, out o' the storm, and should hae been more sensible, it was just the same. We couldna part. I knew that ye wouldna agree if I sent to ask to wed him, since the cattle were taken, so I took the deciding on myself.'

'An' wed a Scot!' said Johnny scornfully, his temper flaring again at what, to him, was inexplicable conduct.

'An' wed a Scot,' returned Helen proudly, 'an' am glad o' it. But I sent the message. I wanted no revenge party coming after me. He knew I sent it. I didna think ye'd come after this long while.'

'I was hurt in the fight,' said Johnny shortly. 'The trail had gone somewhat cold when I got away. And I'd to trace the minstrel to find where ye dwelt.'

'Oh,' said Helen. 'The minstrel! Where is he?'

'South o' here,' said Johnny. 'O' no import to ye.'

They stared at each other fiercely. Childhood quarrels were not so far behind them—the fair boy and the dark girl—for it to seem strange to them to be so at odds, friends again, and then once more crossing spirited wills.

Suddenly Helen's gaze went beyond her brother. He turned and saw a young man standing on the lip of the hollow. It did not need Helen's joyful yet fearful gasp to tell him that this was Alexander Douglas.

CHAPTER 11

In another country

And see ye not yon bonny road
That winds about the fernie brae? ...

As her husband came down the slope he said to Helen:
'One o' the women saw the beggar follow ye. What did he
want? Has he troubled ye?'

'Oh no, Sander,' said Helen breathlessly. 'It is my
brother Johnny come to find me.'

'Why?' said Alexander, stopping in front of Johnny,
looking at him coldly. 'Ye sent the message ye were well.
What need he come?'

He spoke to Helen still, as if Johnny were not present.

Johnny was furious with the words as well as with the
attitude. 'She is my sister,' he snarled. 'Ye kidnapped her.
How should I know but that the message was false? to
keep me home, ye robber!'

Helen said hurriedly: 'No, Sander!' but the Douglas'
hand was already on his dagger hilt.

'He doesna call me that an' I take it quietly,' he said.
Johnny's knife was drawn in the same instant.

They faced each other with hatred in their eyes. It
sparked between them almost tangibly; they shifted and
watched intently, impatient with the heather tangling at
their ankles but neither removing their gaze to glance
down. The sharp scent of the broken stalks rose to their
nostrils. Nor had either the advantage of the sun; it slanted
between them through a small wood of birches on the hillside so that it was slightly shadowed.

'Dinna be fools!' cried Helen. 'What hae ye to quarrel about? Ye should both be satisfied. I shall stay here an' Johnny will be gone. I do not desire either of ye hurt.'

They took no notice of her. Alexander sprang in and Johnny caught his wrist, forcing the hand with the dagger in it upwards, at full stretch. He kept his own right arm that held his dagger at his side, for though the Douglas was wide open for a blow, Johnny suddenly remembered his sister's saying: 'We couldna part.' Heartily as he hated this young man and furious as he was with him, he could not kill him whom his sister loved. Douglas was less scrupulous in his fury; his left hand went to his belt for the second dagger he carried and Johnny was only just in time to drop his own blade and catch his enemy's other wrist. It was as well that he was so quick for there was murder indeed in the other's eyes. But Johnny's right shoulder and arm still had not the strength of the other arm yet, after the wound, and he felt the muscles pull and a strange sense of longing in his arm to drop to rest again, as the pressure became greater and held longer.

As they stood thus, fixed in that tall-armed position until one or the other gave way, Douglas saw a flicker of old pain in the Borderer's eyes. He was in a fury but he recognised that look that did not know it had revealed itself. He said suddenly, unexpectedly: 'Ye are hurt?'

Johnny shook his head savagely, intent on holding the other's attack. But Helen, crouched in the heather, her babe in her arms, her face hidden, looked up and cried: 'He was wounded, Sander, in the raid.'

Alexander stood stock still. Certainly, he had won Helen in that raid; otherwise he was not proud of the memory of a silly jape, and ashamed that there had been injuries, of which he only now heard, and that he had drawn on an injured man.

He opened his fingers and dropped his knives. Johnny

heard them thud to the ground behind him. The Douglas said, with the courtesy most natural to him: 'Ye are more than a match for me, Armstrong. Take it that I yield.'

Johnny stared at him, dumbfounded; he had heard Helen's words only vaguely but now realised that Alexander had acted on them. Looking into his opponent's eyes, Johnny saw that they were warm now, friendly. He was not so boorish as to disregard such generosity and courtesy. He acknowledged it immediately by releasing his grip on the other's wrists, and Alexander stepped back.

Johnny's right arm fell quickly to his side; he felt an enormous physical relief. But he turned and stooped to pick up Alexander's daggers and hand them back to the Douglas with a courtesy equal to the other's.

Alexander thanked him. 'It comes to my mind,' he said, ruefully, 'that we are both maybe too short-tempered.'

The two of them laughed a little. 'It may be so,' agreed Johnny.

Alexander said: 'It was for this confrontation that the beggar sought the Douglas?' It was an amused question. Johnny grinned.

'In some part,' he agreed. 'Most I wished to see Helen.'

As they were speaking, Helen had risen, the child in her arms still, and had come swiftly to them.

' 'Twas almost too much,' she said. 'How could I bear that either of you should die by the other's hand?'

They looked at her shamefacedly, conscious of selfishness; this was also a new experience for them. They had already learnt that dignity did not suffer from generous treatment of an enemy. Both lessons made them grow a little.

The baby gave a little whimper. 'He is hungry,' said Helen. 'I must go back.' She turned for her basket but Alexander picked it up for her and stooped also to gather up the fallen berries. She took basket and fruit under her left arm again—shame for a man to be seen doing woman's work—but he smiled at her softly and she looked back her thanks and her love. Johnny saw all her heart in her eyes but was not now jealous; this was a woman on whom he had no longer any claim. She belonged to the golden boy and the cool uplands of Nithsdale now and Banks would see her no more.

*   *   *

Johnny stayed on in the Douglas stronghold for several days. Helen found fresh clothes for him and, indeed, he was grateful to be free of his rags for a while—they were clean when they were handed back to him before he left and needed some judicious rumpling and soiling in secret before he felt convincing in them again.

In the meanwhile, he hunted with Alexander with enjoyment, on foot, among the low oak woods and in the heather, and quickly learned the skilful use of the spear, a weapon unfamiliar to him. Indeed, the whole society was strange to him—this was not farming as he knew it. The clan pastured a few cattle on the lower, lusher slopes of the hills, where there was grass, and some sheep on the higher land; otherwise, hunting and fishing in the upland pools and fast streams was their livelihood. Also, they used the fruit and materials of the moors.

Helen taught him a little of the Gaelic language that she herself was learning; this was still the customary speech of these western hills—the young men who had found Johnny and brought him to the fort that night had been speaking Gaelic—although many could make themselves understood in the Border tongue that was common to both Englishmen and Scots, with slight variations. These people, though, had never been as involved in the Border warfare as had Johnny's family and others living

along the Wall; they had sometimes come down for pick-
ings, but were mostly content in their hills. The chief and
his son were paramount—respected, loved, at times feared
—but all the people bore the name of Douglas, as if they
were children of the same family; they behaved however,
for all their respectfulness, as if they were grown and equal
children and would engage in any dispute with their chief
on familiar and surprising terms. This amused but impressed Johnny.

He had felt, almost immediately, a strange sense of
having come home. When he was hunting with Alexander
in the high, sweet-smelling hills, he felt it; when, from
those hillsides, in the ringing, blue autumn days, he caught
glimpses of the sea to the west it seemed instantly familiar
—although it was a mysterious horizon to him, straighter
than anything he had ever seen in his life before. He felt
this sense of homecoming again among the people themselves, as if he had lived among them in some distant
dream, as if he belonged with them and would almost be
content to stay. They were quick-tempered and ferocious
when roused but soon kind again, courteous, dignified,
merry. He felt as if he were among kinsmen.

Did Helen feel this also, he wondered, apart from her
love for Alexander Douglas? Watching her among the other
women, at such communal tasks as the berry-picking had
been, or talking easily with the tall men, he saw that she
did. Johnny had forgotten now that he had told Rainault
that probably his mother was of old British blood, driven
to the west by numerous invasions of centuries ago; that
would explain the many sympathies and similarities that
both brother and sister felt. This had slipped both their
memories though; they only noticed the differences and the
likenesses with their own old way of life, and enjoyed
both. These people were as family. Helen's children
would grow up easily here, without divided loyalties.

The clansmen, for their part, accepted Johnny cheerfully and courteously; they already loved Helen for herself, and for the heir that she had brought them, and no one but the three who were concerned knew anything of the abortive fight-to-the-death between Johnny and the chieftain's son.

In the evenings, by firelight, both comfortably tired after the day's hunting, Johnny and Alexander spoke together easily; they had become friends quickly, although Johnny saw that this was not a friendship like that with Rainault, of whom he often thought. He and Alexander would forget each other soon enough, save as brothers-in-law. Nor could Alexander understand Johnny's wanderlust, though ready enough himself to rove from home by day.

'Ye're a married man,' grinned Johnny. 'Who'd be away from home o' nights with Helen waiting your return?'

Alexander laughed, a low and contented but excited laugh. 'Ye'll come to it,' he said, as if in promise.

Johnny saw now what Rainault had meant by his description of the Douglas as Helen's 'golden husband'. His hair and brows were a dark corn-gold and his eyes amber. He was another of the 'western men' that Johnny and Rainault had noticed when they first came into Nithsdale, golder than Johnny himself but with the same bright presence.

To Helen, Johnny spoke quietly one evening of Rainault, for he remembered that the minstrel had said she had been kind to him and that he had told some of his story to her. She seemed fond of him also, and concerned for him. Johnny recalled that she had asked about him before, during their quarrel on the hillside, and that he had rebuffed her unkindly then.

'He looked like a drowned otter when they brought him in from the snow that night,' said Helen, laughing gently at the memory. 'But he was no daunted. Do ye know more of his story, Johnny?'

'I know it all,' said Johnny grimly. 'I hae sworn to aid him in his vengeance.'

They were sitting together on a bench in the shadows, looking towards the cheerful crowd about the fire, Helen upright and graceful, as her life this last year had made her, Johnny with his legs apart, elbows on knees, hands clasped loosely between them.

Helen looked at him doubtfully and worriedly. 'The Armstrong that he seeks sounds formidable.'

'Aye,' said Johnny. 'I surmise that he must be a Liddesdale Armstrong and so we maun go up there, even to Hermitage.'

'He can never slay such a man,' whispered Helen, 'nor ye neither, Johnny. An' even if ye were to succeed, his men would be out like rats an' drag you down.'

'Maybe,' said Johnny, quiet, speculating. 'But I hae sworn.'

The voices of both brother and sister were gentle as they spoke of Rainault. Helen looked at her brother. 'Ye are fond o' the minstrel, as I grew fond o' him, Johnny,' she said. 'I've no heard ye speak so before. Your caring has made ye grow up, as mine for Alexander has made me also. Will ye go back to Banks?' She had sensed her brother's taste for travelling.

'I canna tell,' said Johnny. 'I'm no so keen. But probably needs must. Forbye, I must tell our mother ye are safe.'

'Aye,' said Helen slowly. Then: 'Tell her the bairn is bonny, an' strong. She will be glad to know.'

'Aye,' said Johnny. 'I will tell her. When I go back.'

His sister still looked at him anxiously.

After a while he glanced at her sideways, questioningly. His hair shone bright in the flicker of firelight, his face was composed. Helen disguised her anxiety, smiled at him quickly, and rose to go to her child.

*   *   *

A few days later, Johnny prepared to set off back to Dumfries. He was in his beggar's clothes again though not, for the moment, disguised. The day was wild and autumnal, gold-edged clouds racing across the brown hillsides, the air cool indeed up here in Nithsdale.

Helen stood by the gate of the fort to bid him farewell— the babe was left indoors out of the cold. Her husband, and the three young men who had met Johnny in the heather when he came, were to direct and accompany him down to the track to Dumfries.

The open display of emotion was here accepted, as it was not on the Border; Helen, always naturally affection-ate and expressive, flung her arms about her brother's neck as he turned to say goodbye to her. Johnny, surprised but moved, put his own arms instinctively round her waist and back and was glad to hold her thus. In the very nature of things, their lives were hardly likely to cross again so that neither brother nor sister expected to see each other more. Helen murmured endearments; Johnny, more reticent, yet held her lovingly and dropped a kiss on her forehead.

'Take care, Johnny,' she whispered. He said no more than 'Aye,' and then muttered: 'May ye be always happy, Helen.' Their eyes met for a moment, Helen's filling with tears, then they moved apart. For the first time since she had left Banks, half-excited, half-furious, across Alex-ander's horse, she felt a pang of regretful memory; she had always loved this brother most dearly, for all their battles. But her husband looked across at her and smiled reassuringly and her new life flowed back into

her as the five young men turned now and went out of
the gate.

Johnny, too, felt regret as he moved away; but life was
such in these countries and days that, once separated by
marriage like this, even if not so far apart as were these
two, families had little chance to see a son or daughter
who was living away. And he had fulfilled his vow—found
Helen, found her happy, and left now with an easier heart
and a sense of quiet mockery at his own old notions of
honour before happiness. All was well. Yet he turned at
the foot of the hill to see the last of her green-gowned
figure at the gate.

'She will do well,' said Alexander. 'She is happy here,
Armstrong.'

'Aye,' said Johnny, 'I see that.' He laughed. 'Maybe
your courtship was a mite surprising but I see for myself
now that what others told me is true.' He thought of
Henderson, and Rainault, and even young Wat, worlds
away.

'I shall keep her so,' said Douglas. Johnny nodded in
acknowledgement.

He and the Douglas men parted on the wide track
between the bracken that led back to Dumfries. It was a
parting in friendship. When the Scots had gone back up
the hill, Johnny rubbed fine, dry soil in hair, on face and
hands again, and clothes. Once more he must be the
beggar. But something of the warmth and welcome of the
place and people that he had left remained with him as
he set out to find again the warmth of Rainault and to
fulfil his promise.

CHAPTER 12

To Liddesdale

There's never a stroke comes over thine harp
But it glads my heart within . . .

DUMFRIES town looked grey and cold as he came down towards it from Nithsdale in the greyer weather that had set in after he had parted from Helen; the river was wide here, and fast and full from the first heavy autumn rains in its higher reaches. He wondered fleetingly how he was to find Rainault again. He never doubted that the minstrel would still be here. And indeed he was.

Johnny found him at the hall where they had stayed during their first night in Dumfries, and apparently even more in favour, for he was at the high table, strumming his lute gaily and casually as Johnny came in at the lower end with the other beggars, at the time of the evening meal.

When Rainault was dismissed as the lords and ladies left table, he wandered back down the hall with a strange expression on his face. Johnny wondered at it. As his eyes searched the knot of beggars in the lower hall, he seemed fearful of seeing Johnny among them. But when he did see his friend, his whole countenance lit up with a radiant smile. He elbowed his way through the dingy crowd.

'You are back, *mon ami?*' he exclaimed happily. 'Was she well? And happy? No need for vengeance?'

Johnny's heart had warmed at Rainault's welcome.

'Well, an' happy,' he confirmed, 'an' wi' a baby son!'

Rainault's eyes widened, then he grinned. 'An' the affair of vengeance came to nothing!'

Again Rainault smiled. 'Your heart is at ease now?' he said.

'Aye,' agreed Johnny. 'I'll no trouble Nithsdale more. And what o' ye, my buck?'

Rainault shrugged and smiled but his look of unease returned.

'They have made much of me,' he said, 'would have given me new colours, made me their own minstrel. But I said nay, I could not stay, and I looked always for you.'

'I see ye're glad to see me back,' said Johnny slowly. 'Are ye no a little loth also?'

Rainault flushed. 'I wanted you back, Johnny,' he said. 'I am fond of you.'

'Aye,' said Johnny, 'an' I o' ye. But I put ye in mind overmuch o' your own journey of vengeance, do I no?'

His guess was shrewd. Rainault bit his lower lip but he still held Johnny's gaze firmly, though silently.

Johnny relented. 'Leave it be, lad,' he said. 'Come back to the Wall wi' me for the winter.'

He had never thought he would make such an offer— a man's revenge is his own affair, he had always thought; but he loved Rainault. Revenge seemed insignificant beside this boy's life. Johnny would have loved him no less if he had accepted this way of escape.

But Rainault shook his head. His dark eyes were wide but resigned. 'I must go to Liddesdale,' he whispered. 'I know now that Ill Will's stronghold is in that valley.'

'So,' said Johnny slowly. 'I thought as much. Ye'll no go alone, Rainault.'

It was all that he could offer now.

Rainault smiled, a little wryly, but with a new courage. 'Ah, Johnny,' he said. 'You are a good friend. But I must do this alone in the end. It is my duty. Get you home and tell your mother that Helen is safe and well.'

F

'A' in good time,' said Johnny gruffly. 'Ye'll hae my company up Liddesdale.'

Rainault looked at him in doubt and silence again. Then, when Johnny asked him about the events of their days of separation, he smiled swiftly and shamefacedly at the deliberate change of subject but answered the question with quiet care. 'I have sung the lords and ladies my love songs as they demanded,' he said, 'but I have learned something more of the music of this wild land from the serving-people. They thought that I was scoffing at them when I first asked them to teach me. Then they saw that I wished to know in truth and have been teaching me at whiles. I will tell you more of this some time. But tell me of your venture, Johnny.'

And Johnny laughed infectiously, seeing the irony of it now, and Rainault smiled again, more easily, and with more colour in his face, and was eager to hear what had happened.

'Courteous both,' he said, after Johnny's account of the duel that came to naught.

'I didna feel so at the time,' admitted Johnny, thinking again of his surprise at that unexpected action and generosity on Alexander's part. 'He could hae worsted me wi' ease for my arm was no as strong as I had thought.'

Rainault knew of the wound that Johnny had received in the cattle raid. He had noticed an awkwardness in him at times when they had first met and, having asked about it as they knew each other better, been given a terse account of the incident. He nodded.

'It was hard for your sister to have to watch such a quarrel,' he said. 'Between the two she loved best. A hard thing, *mon ami*.'

'So we saw,' confessed Johnny, 'afterward.'

He told Rainault the rest of his tale and satisfied his curiosity as to the life of the place in the summer—

Rainault remembered only the sodden floor, and huge fires, and the glare of snowdrifts.

During the next few days, Rainault sang him some of the new airs that he had learnt, mostly, it seemed, from one of the kitchen maids, a fair, fine-featured girl called Elspeth. She had come down from a poor homestead in the hills, being an orphan, to work in the castle kitchens for a wage as poor as her life had been before and with little hope of any betterment. She was a kind and courteous girl and, Johnny noticed, looked on Rainault fondly. The minstrel was gentle and sweet-natured with her, as he was with all, and indeed seemed fond of her in return, so that it occurred even to the unromantic Johnny (but he was a more perceptive young man than he had been a week or two ago) that there might be an attachment between them, or that one might develop. Occasionally he came upon them in quiet corners of the castle—Elspeth sitting against a wall, hands clasped round her knees, singing softly in her gentle voice, while Rainault, on one knee, at her side, listened intently, and then felt for the notes she was singing along the strings of his lute.

But Johnny saw also that Rainault's thoughts were often far from this pleasant world of the moment. The Borderer said nothing to him of the errand that was bound to come; an unusual delicacy, that he had learned from Rainault himself, told him to be silent until the minstrel spoke. He knew that he would.

On the third morning, Rainault said quietly, in the gloom of the dawn hall: 'Shall we go on today, Johnny?'

Johnny replied, as quietly: 'Whenever ye're ready, lad.'

Rainault stood up. Johnny saw that his delicate face was pale and looked old. 'There is no virtue in avoiding fate,' he said. 'If you will indeed come with me, Johnny, I will be glad.'

Johnny said, tying his belt: 'My word was as gladly given, as ye know.' Rainault smiled.

'I leave firelight and its embers,' he said, 'and music and the speech of ladies, to take a stony track.' His voice was deliberately light.

'An' Elspeth?' enquired Johnny, also deliberately lightly.

'May she find a good husband,' said Rainault. 'No errant popinjay. No futureless man.' He was laughing now but when Johnny looked at him silently he saw that the minstrel's lightness was self-mocking, and sad.

Then he said something that startled Johnny but touched him also: 'The woman that you love, Johnny Armstrong, will be fortunate. You care for the feelings of others, *mon ami*.'

The remark was not just part of his stock-in-trade, he was never professional in Johnny's company. Now he spoke in all seriousness and the observation was typical of him in its open expression of affection and on matters which Johnny himself would never dream of mentioning.

Johnny grunted. 'My mother was wont to say otherwise,' he said drily. 'Ye're maybe misguided, lad.' Although Rainault's words had surprised, they had not embarrassed him. He was becoming used to Rainault's ways.

But Rainault laughed in earnest now at Johnny's scepticism and refusal to accept compliments.

'Ah, Johnny, Johnny,' he said, 'always so grave. And always thinking the worst of yourself. Do not be so hard on that tall boy from the Border!'

They both laughed, Johnny wryly and Rainault with great fondness.

When they set out some while later, the morning was still and grey; the great mass of Criffell to the west loomed huge above them. A faint mist lay on the low lands in the east to which they travelled. They headed south-east at first, to come to the Solway Firth again and the road which they knew.

The day's journey was mostly in silence, for Rainault refused to let himself chatter in his nervousness and Johnny, while feeling that nervousness in the minstrel and longing to help if he could, had no small talk. However, he thought to ask Rainault what weapons he had. Rainault laughed shortly and drew from his pouch a small, fine-bladed dagger with a red-enamelled hilt. Johnny gasped. 'No other?' he exclaimed, and, when Rainault shook his head: 'Ye'll hae no chance against him wi' that toy!'

Rainault looked at him quizzically. 'What makes you think I have a chance against him with anything other?' he asked.

Johnny groaned. 'Ye should at the least go equally armed,' he said.

Rainault shook his head, both at Johnny's words and at his action now in drawing his own long-bladed knife and offering it to Rainault. 'This I am accustomed to,' said the minstrel. 'Nothing else would serve me any better.'

'Ye only use it for meat and bread,' growled Johnny. 'Ye've no fought wi' it.'

'It will serve,' said Rainault. 'I do not expect to triumph.'

They went on in silence again, the grey tide of the Solway drawing away as fast in the still morning as it had flooded in on that afternoon when they had watched it and Rainault had told his tale. Neither of them noticed it this time. Johnny thought furiously over the situation: no, it was probably not possible that Rainault could defeat his enemy, either with dagger, long knife, or sword; that he could take the revenge he had sworn to take. Why, then, try? Johnny's ideas had indeed changed since he had first met Rainault and offered his help, out of instant liking. His own journey of vengeance had been pointless. He saw that now. There had been nothing to avenge when he had met his sister's happiness. And Rainault's sister was dead, out of the reach of sorrow. What point in the minstrel's throwing his life away for her now?

Johnny said, fiercely: 'Leave it, Rainault. There's no reason, no advantage, in this. Forget the man an' his evil. Come back to Banks wi' me.' This time he meant it more earnestly than before. He stared at Rainault desperately.

But Rainault looked full back at him and said quietly: 'You have changed your tune, *mon ami*. I have sworn, as you had sworn. And because I have been a laggard, there is all the more reason to fulfil my oath at last.'

Johnny growled: 'For a dead girl?'

His deliberate cruelty, which hurt him even as he spoke, was intended to shock Rainault into reality and safety. Rainault, even as his eyes flickered at the wounding words, understood this and smiled crookedly. 'I have sworn,' he said.

No further argument was then possible. They said no more. The tide began to turn again.

*   *   *

Two days later they were back on the banks of the Esk, at the spot where they had previously looked across towards the entrance to Liddesdale. Again it was a still morning, but grey this time, a heavy mist above them, clouding whatever the sky portended.

'There is a ford a little higher,' said Rainault quietly. 'I saw it when we came down before. We need to be on the left bank of the Liddel Water to find the castle of Hermitage.' He knew more, had made more enquiries, than Johnny had realised.

They moved on, alone on the track, found the ford, waded in. The water was icy and took their breath from them. Both were glad to find shallower water, and gravel, beneath their feet. They reached for the alders on the bank to pull themselves up, and wrung what water they could from their clothes.

The Liddel Water was a smaller river than the Esk, and not, at the moment, as fast, for there had been no rain recently in the fells to the north-east out of which it ran. It was grey this morning, and its slower speed seemed somehow ominous. It sucked and gurgled at the roots of the lopped alders on its low banks.

The two young men had spoken little since the first morning of their journey. Rainault was pale, all sophistication had dropped from him. Suddenly, he stopped on the track, doubling over, then turned to the rough grass at the side, and began to vomit. Johnny went to him quickly, holding his forehead in his cupped hand to support the boy as he retched upon an almost empty stomach. Neither felt awkward at this act of tenderness.

When Rainault straightened himself again, wiping his mouth bitterly with the back of a grimy hand, Johnny said: ' 'Twas the shock o' the cold water.'

Rainault looked at him. 'It was fear, Johnny,' he said. 'You know it.'

Johnny returned his gaze. 'Ah, Rainault,' he said, and his eyes were loving as they had been for no other in his life, not even Helen. 'Dinna gang, lad. Come wi' me.'

But Rainault, who had often seemed the younger, the less serious, was now apparently set on his doom and as determined to continue his journey as ever Johnny had been, despite his body's recent involuntary weakness. His smile was as sweet as ever upon Johnny's pleading face but he said: 'I have come so far, Johnny—I must not turn back now. I could not live with myself any more than you could if you were to do the same. I would be indeed a broken man.'

'But living,' said Johnny.

Rainault shook his head. They turned again to the stony track.

CHAPTER 13

Hermitage Castle

Now Liddesdale has long lain in,
There is na ryding there at a' . . .

TOWARDS evening, they knew themselves to be near the
Armstrong stronghold. There were mounted men on the
road ahead, several poor huts about, away from the river's
floodline in winter; they heard voices in the dusk—women
calling children in from the cold, men's harsh voices calling
news.

Johnny had abandoned limp and disguise now and
walked straight, very much present as friend to the slighter
figure of the minstrel. As they rounded a tongue of fell, they
saw, across the fast narrow stream of Hermitage Water,
flowing from the western fells above them to their left, the
black bulk, the torchlit and crowded entrance, of the
great Keep of Hermitage Castle. Johnny heard Rainault
draw in his breath sharply. He laid his own hand on the
hilt of his dagger.

But all was friendly enough. As they forded this stream,
men welcomed the figure of the minstrel, glad of any new
diversion. Several looked with curiosity or suspicion on
the tall figure of his sturdy-beggar companion, but there
could be no harm in one intruder. Also, he had the look
of an Armstrong about him, for all his ragged gear. No
questions were asked.

The great double gates, two storeys high, the outer of
bog oak as hard as iron, the inner of iron itself, bound and
studded and impregnable, stood open. The men on guard,

under the guttering torches, knew all who entered, or knew them harmless. Beyond the guardrooms, the hall glowed with welcome golden warmth, and the vagrants— a few other beggars as well as Rainault and Johnny—were not kept as far from the flames as in other, more pretentious halls. Here there was indeed what they had not expected—hospitality, good fellowship, even the rough kindness of men who live in hard places and know a common cause. Both were surprised.

From their place beyond the great fireplace Rainault and Johnny watched the table being set up along the hall for the evening meal and the lord and lady of Hermitage come in, with their household and their guests.

'That is not he,' whispered Rainault, with a dry mouth, as the Armstrong, the laird of Liddesdale, took his place at the high table. Then, as the guests, mostly men, followed, he gasped: 'That one, Johnny, that one!' The tall, laughing figure of a dark Armstrong was the object of his frantic whisper and lifted hand.

'Hush ye,' said Johnny. 'Ye can do naught here.'

He watched the man closely. He was big and confident, his clothes of good, hard quality, a man used to mastery. It seemed ludicrous that Rainault should think to challenge him. But a glance at Rainault's face showed him that remembered hatred possessed the young minstrel with strength and courage. He ate well as their food was brought to them and stood up without a moment's hesitation or nervousness as the minstrel that men had noticed in the company was called upon to sing.

His bitter-sweet songs followed the very different, harsher declamation of the hall's resident musician. Tonight Johnny found Rainault's music more deeply moving than he had ever done before. The setting made it all the more poignant.

Men applauded loudly when he had done. The Hermi-

tage musician bore Rainault no animosity for the difference in their offerings and grinned at him, gap-toothed, as
he stepped down. Rainault paused and generously dropped
some of the money he had been given for his own singing
into the other's hand as he made his way back to Johnny.

'He did not recognise me,' he hissed. 'He looked at me
but was so busy with food and boasting—and drink, that
he did not even see me, I think.'

Johnny nodded. He beckoned to one of the serving-men
nearby and the lad, in his greasy clothes, came, at the
lifted hand, as if one of his masters had summoned him.
Something about the beggar told his instinct that the
ragged clothes were disguise.

'Tell us o' the company,' said Johnny. 'Who is laird o'
what hall? When do they go?'

The boy indicated this one and that in the flickering
light of the fire and the torches; Johnny nodded, betraying
no especial interest in any, and accepted as calmly the
news that the dark Armstrong was laird of a hall north-
west of Hermitage and would be riding on the morrow as
he accepted the news that another, pursy, member of the
clan, who lived to the east, was not due to leave for three
days. Rainault passed a coin to Johnny and he passed it
to the serving-lad who thanked him and left.

Johnny turned and looked at Rainault. The minstrel
was strangely flushed. 'We leave early,' he said, 'and wait
in the hills.'

'Aye,' said Johnny heavily, 'an' ye'll have it so.'

'You have given me strength to get here,' said Rainault,
suddenly tender. 'Get you home, Johnny.'

But Johnny shook his head. The inevitability of the
coming conflict between Rainault and Ill Will appalled
him. The only thing that he could do now was to stay by
Rainault and try to assist him in the actual event. His
imagination worked more vividly on Rainault's probable

fate than ever it had done on his own if Douglas had worsted him in their Nithsdale duel; he swallowed hard, and his stomach was cold.

They sat on silently, watching the company at the high table, Ill Will the loudest, the most striking of them all. 'So, he drew her,' said Rainault bitterly, and again, as he had said before of his dead sister: '*Ma pauvre.*'

Will Armstrong's hair gleamed chestnut in the torch-light, his fine teeth glinted as he laughed hugely; he could be courtly also, leaning to the lady of the hall, on his left, as she spoke. Johnny watched him with cold eyes. He wondered if he remembered Rainault's sister. Probably he had not even cared that much. The world lay wide to such a man as this.

CHAPTER 14

The encounter

And, fingers five, get up belive:
And, manhood, fail me naught!

NOT until Johnny and Rainault waited at the gate to leave the castle the next morning, did they realise that the darkness they had taken to be just that of a dark day, inside the tall hall, was due to a heavy mist, flat on the fells.

They paused, uncertain for a moment. Then, as the guard motioned them on impatiently, Johnny asked the direction of the hall the serving-lad had mentioned the night before as being that of Ill Will. One of the men indicated a track into the fells, visible for only a few yards in that clinging mist. Johnny nodded in thanks. He turned to Rainault and saw, to his amazement, that, even in this fateful moment, the minstrel was instinctively covering his lute against the damp. Rainault caught his glance and smiled wanly. 'My livelihood,' he said. And then: 'My livelihood, *mon ami.*'

Johnny loved him the more for his pale joke in the teeth of death.

They stepped out into the mist.

'We shall not see him for this accursed weather,' said Rainault anxiously. Johnny saw that now that he had made up his mind as to the pattern that events were to follow, he was impatient of any delay.

Johnny said: 'There seems but the one track. I think we'll no' miss him.' He would have been happier if he could have thought that they might miss Ill Will's home-going. The moment of doom might be postponed for just that little longer, despite Rainault's acceptance of fate.

They climbed the hill north-west of Hermitage. The dampness of the air clung all about them, on skin, hair, clothes.

'Do no be too courteous,' growled Johnny, 'if ye mean to challenge him alone thus. Watch both his hands.' He remembered Alexander Douglas' ploy.

'As you say, Johnny,' replied Rainault, but Johnny, despairingly, was not sure that he had even heard the advice. His expression was absent, his head turned to listen.

They stopped over the brow of the hill and stood to-gether, shivering a little with the cold, or with apprehen-sion. They did not speak. Rainault took the coral-handled dagger from his pouch and thrust it through his belt. Johnny groaned at sight of it but Rainault shook his head, smiling at his friend. This action of putting the knife ready seemed to give him composure. He laid his lute, in its leather wrapping, carefully among the tufted grass and stood to listen and look, straining his ears and eyes into the mist. Johnny saw, with a sinking heart, that look of doom upon Rainault's face that had so chilled him when he had first seen it the day that they had looked up to-wards Liddesdale from Eskdale, on their first journey together.

Presently they heard the slow, sodden thud of hooves as a band of horsemen mounted the wet hillside. Johnny winced. He had known that Armstrong would not travel alone but now the company—clansmen all—seemed ominous and too immediate.

Yet Rainault stood forward boldly and hailed his enemy, riding among his men.

'Ill Will Armstrong!' he called. 'Dismount! I have a score to settle with you.'

Ill Will reined in, astonished.

' 'Tis the minstrel,' said one of his men scornfully. 'Last night's sweet singer!'

Still Armstrong stared. Then he said, with a harsh laugh: 'I kenned I minded your face somehow. The French wench's brother! What d'ye hae to say to me, my pretty boy?'

Rainault spat into the rough grass towards the Armstrong, staring at him through the shifting mist that made the figures of the mounted men loom and dim in turn.

'She is dead, Ill Will,' he said. 'Because of you she killed herself. That is the score that I wish to settle.'

Ill Will's followers laughed. One of them swung himself down. 'I'll deal wi' the popinjay for ye, Will,' he said.

But Will Armstrong had also dismounted. Johnny had seen surprise in his face at Rainault's words, but neither regret nor guilt. 'Nay,' he said now, 'this is my game. I never liked the boy. Keep ye an eye on that other.'

Johnny's knife was out as soon as Rainault's but neither had the reach of the long swords that the two men had drawn. Ill Will's man set the wide point of his blade at Johnny's throat and he had to stand, powerless.

But Rainault, with a swift and surprising movement and more knowledge of knife play than Johnny had known he possessed, had ducked within the length of Ill Will's blade as the man's arm straightened and, although he was not in time to get right through Armstrong's guard, the coral pommel of Rainault's knife held the hilt of the glinting sword and the moment was, amazingly, one of deadlock.

The unexpected strength of Rainault's arm forced the man sideways in his sword grip and Rainault, also, was turned so that Johnny, clenching his hands in frustration and despair, saw the boy's fine-boned profile. Astonishingly, there was a look of calm fierce joy on the minstrel's face. Johnny knew that Rainault did not expect to emerge from this encounter alive but he saw that, for this brief poised moment at least, Rainault was experiencing the sharp satisfaction of holding his enemy.

So they stood, tense against each other, the tall man in the prime and strength of his manhood, and the boy not yet done growing.

Then, even as Johnny called out frantically: 'Mind ye his other hand, Rainault!' the Armstrong reached down swiftly for his hunting knife, drew it from his belt, and thrust it upwards into Rainault's slanted body, twisting it, as one would gralloch a deer. Rainault, with one hard indrawn breath of shock, went down like a stone, to writhe slowly and silently in the wet grass.

As Johnny started forward in fury, the sword at his throat drew blood. He stopped.

'Ye butcher!' he cried. 'Ill Will indeed, to kill so foully!'

Armstrong looked across at him, grinning, sheathing his unused sword, stooping to thrust his bloodied knife into the soil to cleanse it.

'An' who are ye to call names, my gallant?' he enquired grimly.

'An Armstrong,' cried back Johnny, wild with grief, 'an' shamed to bear the name!' He spat towards the man, as Rainault had done.

'Shall I blood him, Will?' asked the man who held him at sword-point.

'Nay,' said Armstrong, turning to his horse, 'I've no quarrel wi' the younker. An Armstrong, eh? What did ye in company wi' a French bastard, eh?'

He was mounted, turning his horse, sneering at Johnny.

'I kept better company then than I hae ever kept

before,' cried Johnny. 'Ye murderer! Ye blackguard! The name o' Armstrong stinks!'

The Armstrong holding him in check growled but Ill Will only grinned cruelly.

'Come ye away, Jock,' he said. 'We hae wasted over-much time a'ready.'

Again he turned his horse and, as this Jock backed away from Johnny's still ready knife and reached his horse and sheathed his sword and mounted, the whole band turned away and were lost immediately in the mist.

Johnny, thrusting his blade back in his belt, ran to Rainault. The slow writhing had ceased. Rainault was dead.

Sobbing bitterly, unashamed of these tears of love and fury, Johnny gathered the limp, still warm body into his arms and bent to kiss the brow quite smoothed by death and to pass a gentle hand over the half-closed eyes to close them forever.

'I had sooner died than ye,' he said aloud, passionately and truthfully, though hardly hearing his own words. The ugliness, stupidity, and waste of this death confused him with anger.

Presently he raised himself, laying Rainault's body gently down as if the boy might still feel the earth hard beneath him. He stood up, the tears dried stiff on his face, and turned to look for the dead boy's dropped knife. He found it and brought it back, to twist it into Rainault's girdle and jerkin to make a sop for the dark blood that welled from the wickedly-dealt wound. Then he picked up and slung the shrouded lute over one shoulder and once again stooped to gather Rainault into his arms.

He stood looking down into the still, golden face that lay against his arm. Death had removed all expression from it save an inborn twist of the sweet mouth, as if the

G

familiar smile might suddenly break again. Mist beaded
brilliantly the dark hair. There was an unearthly look
about the dead boy.

So, thought Johnny. No doubts, no hesitations when it
came to it. No faintheart, after all, my friend. I will avenge
you, Rainault the Breton, and your dead sister.

He walked steadily back down the track to Hermitage,
carrying his burden carefully. The mist swirled wide and
tall about him, like the ghosts of men. The faint breath
of a coming wind already moved upon the hillside.

The men on duty at the gate recognised him. They came
from the postern gate with exclamations. 'Who did this?'
they asked, unusually shocked by death; but Rainault had
been noticed and liked by all the previous evening, for his
gentleness and courtesy and the eloquence of his fingers
among the strings of his lute. 'Killing's out o' fashion now,'
said one, with a grim but not unkind humour.

Johnny said briefly: 'There was bad blood atween him
and yon Armstrong.' He jerked his head over his right
shoulder in the direction that Ill Will and his band had
taken. Another of the men said: 'Yon's an ill fellow to
cross.'

'Aye,' said Johnny grimly. 'So 'tis proven. Where may
I bury him?'

One man went back to ask permission of the castle;
another went to fetch a shroud and a spade. Presently
they returned and led Johnny along the bank of Hermitage
Water to higher ground where there were small crosses
almost sunken in the dying grass. A priest followed the
armed men, muttered a perfunctory prayer over the
stiffening body, and then he and the men returned to
the castle, he to a warm fire, they to their watch.

Johnny buried Rainault's lute with him; it seemed right
that he should do so. He was calm with sorrow now. Only,
as he piled the last spadefuls of earth into Rainault's

grave, he was suddenly shaken for a moment by the realisation that he would now never see that gay smile again nor hear that light, careful voice. This death had changed the world indeed for Johnny Armstrong of Banks and that world only a few months old.

CHAPTER 15

Through the Waste

O Lord, what is this worldis bliss
That changeth as the moon!

IN the short space of that evening—very short, for though the mist moved and lifted a little, it soon enveloped the land again—Johnny got clear of Liddesdale, striking across the lie of the valley up into the eastern fells. He felt that he must be far from the place where he had been known with Rainault and where he had buried him. His one aim now was to collect his sword and his horse from the care of Robbie Henderson, to tell his mother of Helen's well-being, and then to return for vengeance. All he wanted now was the death of Ill Will. If he himself were to die immediately after at the hands of the Armstrong clan, so be it. He had not men enough at his command to make a foray into Liddesdale and hope to slay his enemy and then ride back unscathed.

His jerkin was stiff with Rainault's blood that had soaked it as he had carried him to burial; his throat throbbed from the cut that the Armstrong's blade had inflicted as Johnny had started forward at Rainault's killing. Blood from that wound also had dripped on to his clothes. If he noticed any of these things it was only as reminders of the work to be done.

The dead boy haunted him through the black night. I would have roamed the world with you for company, he thought, and been content. And we could not even say farewell. His mourning was deep indeed. Only now did he

realise that Rainault's joyous coming into his life had
released in him a gentleness and sense of humour that he
had never realised he possessed. He felt that, likely, these
would now depart with the death of Rainault. He felt no
gentleness that night. Nor did his wanderlust mean anything more to him now that Rainault could no longer
share his journeyings. I set out with such glee, he thought;
better have stayed, like an animal, at home. But then he
would never have known Rainault's courtesy and affection and would have been the poorer. Their destruction
must be avenged though, he knew that; he could not
merely enjoy their memory and let that suffice. His own
life mattered little to him now. Even the memory of
Helen in the hills was fading. But his mother must be told.

He rested a while, sometime about midnight, crouching
with his back against a cairn, half-way up to the tops of
Bewcastle Waste. He was unfamiliar with the bogs and
the banks up there and was not going to risk long night
travelling with his revenge untaken. But dawn saw him
on his way again, with a long stride through the mist that
no beggar would use. At mid-morning though, the mist
suddenly thinned, and lifted, and cloudless blue sky was
revealed. One of the short spells of late, unnatural summer
set in, common to these lands. He glanced back the way
he had come, once, briefly, and saw a silver gleam amongst
the dark country below. He was puzzled by it for a moment,
then realised that it was sunlight on the Solway Firth, and
turned his face forward again, moved by memory but in-
flexible in purpose.

Now he was on the very tops of the Bewcastle Waste. It
lay before and all about him, and it was beautiful, as he
had never thought it before. Bracken burned with colour
in that autumn brilliance of light, the bogs glinted without
malice, the streams could be heard in a joyous noise even
where they were invisible in the many deep little valleys,

still green with summer. He saw a distant peel-tower, sheep wandering and grazing without a shepherd, no other signs of man. Hatred, enmity, murder, seemed impossible and inconceivable in that innocent air.

*   *   *

When Johnny came down from the north, two days later, to the Henderson homestead, he found Robbie in the yard. One of the Henderson horses had gone lame and Robbie was superintending its treatment.

The yard and timbers and roof were steaming in the low and brilliant sunlight of this still-enduring Saint Martin's summer, and, as Robbie straightened from examining the horse, the light shone full in his eyes so that he did not, at first, recognise the tall ragged boy who had been admitted to the yard and was coming towards him. Then the hair—free now of ash and peat-dust after the mist and the last few nights' dews—and the vivid serious eyes identified Johnny to him.

'So ye're back,' observed Robbie calmly. 'I grant I'd no thought to see ye again.'

'I hae come to thank ye, for the care o' my horse an' other gear,' said Johnny, 'an' to take them again.'

No more.

Robbie stared at him. 'Ye found Helen?' he asked.

He saw the great brown stain of dried blood on the faded jerkin but saw that Johnny himself was not wounded. He said nothing of it.

Johnny seemed to have to stir himself from a waking dream to hear and answer Robbie's question.

'Aye,' he said. 'Aye. I am sorry. Yon part o' the quest was successful.'

'What else?' enquired Robbie shrewdly. 'More has occurred to ye than that. What o' the minstrel?'

'I found him,' said Johnny, closing his eyes for a moment. 'I found him. He was o' help.'

Robbie did not ask any more questions. He saw that Johnny was grateful, that he wished to assure those who had tried to help him that their advice had been useful, but also that something more than journeying and seeking and finding had moved and somehow changed him.

He took the boy indoors and got out, from the great chest where the Hendersons' few changes of clothing were kept, his precious padded jacket, and another pair of breeches and a clean shirt.

'These are no mine,' said Johnny dazedly.

'Nay,' laughed Robbie, 'ye left yours wi' my cattle lad.'

'Aye, I mind me,' said Johnny. 'But I canna take yours.'

'Ye can hardly take your own back from the lad,' laughed Robbie. 'Ye'd no know them now.'

Johnny acquiesced, thanking him quietly. He agreed to wait for the return of Robbie's father, who was away to market; he knew that he must do this, in duty bound, to thank the man for his help, to give him news.

So he spent the day about the Henderson homestead, glad to be in his own boots and jacket again, and tending to his own horse. His rags were burned. And Robbie brought, from the recesses of his own wall-bed, Johnny's sword, wrapped in soft cloth and well cared for.

Johnny took this with great gratitude and more animation than Robbie had yet seen in him. His fingers closed firmly about the hilt, he balanced and measured the blade with a satisfied and savage look about his mouth.

Robbie said: 'Ye mean to use it, Armstrong?'

Johnny responded swiftly, his eyes meeting Robbie's questioning gaze with certainty.

'I mean to use it,' he said. 'An' on another Armstrong if I've the chance.' He said no more and Robbie too was silent, seeing that here there were things the Armstrong wished to brood upon privately.

When Henderson returned, late in the short afternoon, beneath a menacing sky streaked from the north-east with high coral and cobalt feathers of cloud—very different from the still cool evenings of recent days—Robbie met him as he dismounted, and told him of Johnny's return.

Henderson whistled in surprise, turning to unstrap his saddlebag. 'Yon's a man I never truly thought to see again,' he said.

'It *is* a man that he's returned,' said Robbie, taking the halter of his father's horse, 'and no the boy that he went. He'll maybe tell *ye* what's happened.'

' 'Tis his affair,' said Henderson. 'Much may make men o' boys. Seeing the world, an' maybe death. Maybe a death that touched close.'

He was a shrewd man. Johnny, meeting him again, remembered how shrewd and felt that he guessed the emotion within his guest. They greeted each other warmly, for Henderson had liked the boy and Johnny remembered, now, how much the man had sympathised with his longing in the spring.

'I guess ye found the little maid hale an' hearty?' said Henderson, glad to be sitting at his own table and of the comfort of his own hall, as night drew on. He saw in Johnny's eyes what Robbie had meant by saying that he had gone a boy and returned a man.

Johnny laughed, shortly, for the first time in many days, remembering his stay in Nithsdale, though it seemed so long ago.

'No maid!' he said. 'She has a son, a child o' promise as far as *I* may tell.'

Henderson laughed. 'So!' he said. 'Satisfactory! An' she is happy?'

'Aye,' replied Johnny, sitting beside him as he ate. 'I

had meant to intrude. But I didna do so. They were happy together.'

'So that's no your trouble,' said Henderson. 'I see your hand ready to your hilt though. But I'll no ask.'

Johnny, leaning forward on the table, in the firelight, frowned. 'I would tell ye,' he said, 'an' I would hae told Robbie if I could. But 'tis something I dinna seem able to say. I hae a duty laid on me that will take me back to Liddesdale though.'

'To your kinsfolk?' asked Henderson, watching the young face turned sideways from him. He saw the mouth harden.

'I would disclaim the name o' Armstrong an I could,' said Johnny.

His voice was so grim that Henderson said: 'Men dinna always do wrong from choice.'

'That one did,' said Johnny savagely. 'I canna tell ye.' He looked at Henderson with apology and despair in his eyes. The older man put a hand on his shoulder for an instant.

'The cattle went back,' he said, changing a subject that, he saw, bit too sharp and deep for more words. If Helen were well, then something else had happened on that journey that had destroyed the happy and thoughtless wanderlust that Henderson had recognised in Johnny in the spring. Likely a death, after all, he thought.

'An' I sent the full money for yon Hugh,' he said. Johnny, astonished to remember a life and people that seemed in another world, made an effort and thanked him and tried to think and speak of these other things.

When Sim swaggered in some twenty minutes later, Johnny barely noticed him and he meant nothing to him. Yet he noticed young Wat following his brother, now six months taller and broader and grinning a welcome that Johnny returned. He will be like Robbie, he thought, and

was amazed at his own perception, who had never before
taken much thought of or care for others. And Henderson
and Robbie are good men, as Wat will be, and I thought
them once my enemies; but my real enemy is my kinsman
and him I will kill if I can. And no one really matters to
me now save a dead boy buried on a hillside in Liddesdale.

During the evening meal, he was forcibly reminded of
Elspeth as the women brought in the food. He thought of
her sadly. But Rainault had not expected to return, he
said to himself; he'll have given her no cause to think that
he would, just otherwise in fact. She may have cried,
Johnny thought unhappily; but she'll forget him in time,
with luck. He wished the girl well, kind for her because she
had been kind for Rainault.

When the tables were removed, Johnny stood talking
to Wat, who was as cheerful as ever, flattered to be treated
as an adult by this guest whom he had liked at his first
visit in the spring. This time though, Wat noticed, there
was an air of sorrow about him that impressed the
younger boy. And when Sim approached them, with mischief in his mind, intending to make some malicious
remark about beggars, or untaken revenge (for he had
been quick to gather something of the story), Wat guessed
his intention and turned on his brother before he could
speak. 'Awa' wi' ye, Sim,' he said, risking a blow round
the head for his impudence, but determined to protect
Johnny from insult.

But Sim had seen the look in Johnny's eyes—an
authority of experience and a precarious anger—and,
though he scowled at Wat and then pretended haughtily
not to notice the warning, he moved thankfully enough
away. He saw that the Armstrong was no man to meddle
with now.

CHAPTER 16

Homecoming

. . . I saw a dead man win a fight
An' I think that man was I.

BY the morning, the threat of the previous night's stormy
sunset was being fulfilled and that last frail misleading
flash of summer was gone. A north-east wind blew steadily
above the valley in which the Henderson farm lay, and
thick ragged clouds raced across the sky which yesterday
had been so kindly.

Johnny was to set off early for Banks; the journey would
take almost all day in any case. But he wanted to be back
there with his news and then on his way to Liddesdale
again as soon as possible. Longer thinking would but make
the future seem even harder. So, booted and cloaked, he
bade a grateful farewell to the Hendersons in the grey
dawn. Henderson and Robbie came to the gate to see him
go.

'This time we'll no see him back, for sure,' observed
Henderson grimly.

Robbie looked at him. 'Did he tell ye aught?' he asked.

Henderson shook his head. 'Nay,' he said. 'Whatever it
was that happed on that journey, it hurt overmuch to
tell.'

Robbie said: 'There was blood on his clothes when he
came back. It wasna his.'

Henderson nodded. 'A death then,' he said, 'as I thought.
An' he's on his way to Liddesdale for vengeance. No man
comes out o' that alive.'

'He seeks an Armstrong,' said Robbie.

'Aye?' said his father. 'Yon makes the end more certain then.'

Grimly, but with liking and sadness, they watched the rider move up the hill in the louring weather, then turned, silently, to the day's activities.

*   *   *

It was reivers' weather again when Johnny returned to Banks. By mid-morning, a thin cold rain began to fall, which soon became heavier and faster, mixed with sleet, and driven almost horizontally on a furious wind. Johnny became sharply aware of the dark line of the Wall through the sleet, like a heavy thought not to be shaken off. This was familiar ground, known so well in the spring and in the years before that, but no part of the last six months. A terrible sense of loneliness blew around Johnny with that bitter wind from the north-east. He knew, now, something of the country from which it came, the treeless, sea-fret-haunted fells above Teviotdale and Tynedale where he had wandered in search of Rainault and Rainault had wandered, just before him, in more desultory search of his sister's betrayer. And as the wind brought memories of that search and therefore of Rainault into his mind, so it also brought the reality of the loss of Rainault. His eyes stung with more than the tears that the icy wind forced from them if he incautiously turned his head; vividly he remembered those few golden days in Nithsdale when they had both been so free for a while of the pressures of their various searches and revenges. He should have come back with me, he thought violently, longingly. Then the dream's impossibility was quite clear to him again and he rode on without any more illusions.

By mid-afternoon, his cloak and the back of his jacket

were soaked, and darkness was drawing on quickly. Still the sleet and rain streamed from the north-east. He was nearing Banks. I wonder how good a watch they keep, he thought sardonically.

He was riding now across the flat hilltop land to the east of Banks that he had always used for grazing, and the walls of the homestead showed occasionally, black and featureless, through the blown curtain of sleet. This was home. He was suddenly surprised to realise that he was glad to be back. But this time it will not be wanderlust that takes me away again, he thought.

Good lookout *was* being kept. As he approached the gates, a voice that was unmistakeably Jock's called out: 'Who gang's there?'

Johnny, grinning to himself, called back: 'A' right, Jock, lad, 'tis Johnny Armstrong!'

Even with the whistle of wind round his ears, he heard the exclamation of surprise and delight, and the gates were pulled rapidly open. He rode in, blinking at spluttering torchlight, and, thankfully, heard the gates slam to behind him and felt the respite from the storm. And then Jock was at his side, his face creased with welcome: 'I never thought to see ye again, lad! My, but you're sodden!'

Johnny swung himself down from his saddle.

'Reivers' weather again, Jock, my lad,' he said, cheerfully, warmed by the pleasure in the old man's face.

Jock looked puzzled for a brief moment, then remembered the events of that day of rain and sleet a year ago. 'Oh aye,' he said. 'Yon was the start. Ye've found her then?' He guessed that Johnny would not have spoken thus had his search been a failure and he was pleasurably surprised at the assurance and humour in Johnny's voice.

'Aye,' said Johnny, standing now in the shelter of the door of the stables and pulling off his dripping cloak. 'An' I've a nephew, Jock!' He was surprised at the pleasure he

suddenly felt at the thought of that flaxen babe in Nithsdale.

The old man took his cloak, laughing. 'The golden lad
that took her?' he asked. 'I'm no surprised.'

'Aye,' said Johnny. 'I'll in an' tell my mother.'

As he went across the yard, the cheerfulness and feeling
of homecoming began to fade. The sense of loneliness and
inescapable fate returned. On such a day, a year ago, if
he had set better guard, Helen would not have been
snatched, he would not have set out on his subsequent
search for her, nor met and lost Rainault, nor be on his
way now to his death. He was quite hard-headed about
his fate. He had no illusions about that either. But all
seemed bitterly ironic now, after speaking to Jock so
cheerfully.

As he went in at the lower door of the tower, two of the
household men, who were stacking stores by torchlight,
turned to see who had come in, recognised him, and
greeted him with surprise and—to Johnny's astonishment
—with pleasure. He had always known, vaguely, that Jock
was fond of him, had not thought that any other, save his
mother, might be.

At the head of the curving stone steps to the upper hall
stood Jamie. As Johnny went up, he looked at his younger
brother with a sudden shock of surprise, knowing who he
was but hardly recognising this tall, serious young man,
with the smudge of dark hair on his top lip, as the boy
whom he had left in charge of household and farm six
months ago; Jamie did not recognise his elder brother at
all until he spoke, wondering fiercely who this intruder
was, shadowed by the torches below and with so hard a
face, lines bitten deep at the sides of his mouth. Then
Johnny said: 'Ye've done well, lad. I see I made no
mistake.'

He saw recognition, pleasure, disappointment, all cross

his brother's face fleetingly. He went on, amusedly, before
Jamie could even exclaim at realising who this was: 'I've
no come back to take over again, lad. Dinna fear! I'm
awa' again in the morning.'

But Jamie, guiltily conscious of having shown how
much he had relished his command, how little he wanted
to relinquish it, broke in: 'Welcome home, Johnny. We
feared ye were lost.'

Johnny was beside him by now; they were of an equal
height. The elder brother smiled. Then he said: 'I've no
wish to startle our mother. Go an' prepare her, lad. But
tell her I'm no stopping.'

Jamie opened the hall door behind him and went into
the sudden light of flames and torches, leaving the door
ajar. A moment later, Johnny pushed the door wide and
stood on the threshold of the glowing, smoky hall—a
north-east wind always drove the smoke back down the
chimney, he remembered sharply. His mother was looking
incredulously and expectantly towards the door—Jamie
had just spoken to her—but no one else expected him and,
for a moment, there was a stunned silence as they all
looked at this tall young man with the striking appearance,
whom they had almost forgotten, who had come so surprisingly into their evening. Then there was a sudden
hubbub of welcoming voices. The dogs that he thought
would have forgotten him during a whole summer came
fawning to his hands. Griselda jumped up from her
mother's side and, as impulsive as Helen had ever been,
ran round the tables to her brother, not expecting any
response to her wild greeting but too glad to remain still.

Johnny, touched by the warm welcome of the household
and then by his little sister's tearful and loving face,
swung her up unexpectedly into his arms and spoke so
kindly to her that she clung round his neck with the
greatest joy that she had ever felt. Then he set her down

gently, took her by the hand, and, nodding smilingly at
the noisy tables, made his way to his mother and stooped
to kiss her forehead.

She was calm but her eyes shone with questions.

'Helen is safe an' well, mother,' he said, pulling off his
wet jacket. Thomas came up to take it from him and to
set it by the hall fire to dry. Johnny thanked him, smiling
at the tall boy that he had grown. Then he sat on the
bench by his mother. 'She is wed an' has a son,' he went
on. 'I was bid to tell ye that he is a strong an' a bonny
bairn an', indeed, I saw that for myself.'

His mother nodded and smiled happily. Thomas and
Griselda came close to listen to all that was said and even
Jamie remained. Johnny had a sudden terrible feeling that
it was Rainault who stood there, so like was the colouring
and the first fine beard. He realised now that that was what
had so startled him when he first saw Jamie at the top of
the steps in the lower hall. Then the uncanny feeling was
gone again; it was only his brother who stood there. The
sense of emptiness returned.

His mother's questions roused him. 'Where hae ye been,
Johnny? Where *is* Helen?'

'A good few miles,' he replied. 'Fells north-west o' Dumfries. Wife of a chief's son an' the babe heir after his
father. She's happy. No doubt o' that.'

Again his mother nodded. She was reassured on that
score now. She felt a change in Johnny though, that none
of the others really noticed, for he seemed not much more
talkative than he had ever been, although his kindness
to Griselda had delighted his sister and rather surprised
everyone else for the moment; but his mother caught a
glimpse, or thought she did, of a gentleness and even a
gaiety that she had never known before in her eldest son.
She saw also a new air of grim self-assurance. She chose
to ignore that for the moment and spoke to the gentler

Johnny with a loving mockery that she had very rarely been able to use with him.

'So our family honour is safe?' she said softly. But the tone was so like Rainault's gentle teasing that Johnny winced. 'Aye,' he answered brusquely.

His mother thought that she had been mistaken in her judgement and was silent.

Johnny was suddenly ashamed of the tone in which he had spoken—it had not been ungraciousness on his part, although he realised that his mother could not know that. He suddenly remembered again how she had spoken to him in the spring, when he had set out, of her own longing to travel; he resolved to try to make up for the apparent harshness of his answer just now by telling her something of his travels.

He looked sideways at her. She sat silent, hurt by that response to her teasing. When he spoke now she was startled, for this *was* that new Johnny after all, confiding, eloquent, obviously trying to please her. He said: 'I went on my travels as a beggar, mother.'

She turned quickly at the soft tone, the unexpected confidence. He smiled into her wide eyes and felt some reward for his attempt in her interested surprise.

'An' another surprise for ye,' he went on, gently. ' 'Twas at the suggestion o' Henderson himself! An honourable man, mother, an' wi' at least two honourable sons. Hugh never saw that. Perhaps he couldna. Those that raided us were the wilder boys, I ken that now. Ye had the cattle back? an' the money for Hugh?'

'Aye,' said his mother. 'I was taken aback somewhat.'

'He said he would make recompense,' said Johnny. 'I'll grant that that surprised me too. But he's an honourable man. An' I only learned that by asking for advice in my search for Helen! 'Twas he suggested I go as a beggar to find the minstrel who kenned the way.'

H

'A beggar!' repeated his mother, still trying to see her self-important son in such a guise.

Now Johnny grinned, no longer the conceited young man that he had once been. 'There was no much choice,' he said. 'Men would hae looked askance at jacket an' sword an' the good clothes o' your making.'

'Aye,' said his mother, 'maybe.' She hesitated, wanting to ask more, not wanting to anger him nor lose this new kindness. She wondered why her first light-hearted remark had evoked that sharp response but dared not ask.

Johnny saw her hesitation and understood it. He was angry with himself and felt guilty that she should be so wary of him now. He could not explain. He determined to go on with his account even though he could not bear to mention Rainault in it.

'I learned from Henderson that Helen was likely northwest o' here, though I wandered the Border whiles—a poor beggar! an' no very convincing, I surmise!—till I came on more certain clues. 'Tis rich land, mother, or has been, an' will be again. Richer than our fells! Then I turned for Dumfries, side the Solway Water—' he paused, remembering. 'A grand town, mother. I'd no seen the like.' He gave her more description of the shops, houses, people. Her eyes sparkled unwontedly as she listened. Something of this she had seen herself, in towns, long ago. The smoky hall troubled her.

Then Johnny continued: 'We set on up Nithsdale to seek Helen. That's no the same as fell-farming neither. Huntsmen, herdsmen. But grand folk. An' Helen happy, mother. She's happy. She would hae been glad for ye to see the bairn.' His mother nodded, dreaming. She had sensed quickly that Johnny had omitted someone from his tale. She asked no questions. She thought of her daughter, and of a grandson far from her, whom she would

never see, but who would continue the family. And then
Johnny turned to her happy face.

'I'm no staying, mother,' he said gently. 'Did Jamie no
tell ye?'

The light went from her face. She shook her head.

'Ah, I gave him no time,' said Johnny, with soft
apology. 'I am sorry. I followed in too hard on his
heels.' He introduced a rough humour into his voice:
'The welcome's good but I'll no take the farm from Jamie
again.' Then he added, quietly: 'An' I've other business on
hand.'

His mother was not able to respond to the spark of
humour, and his last words frightened her. 'What other
business?' she asked fearfully. 'Oh, Johnny, ye've
changed!'

'For the better?' he asked wryly. 'It couldna be for the
worse!'

Again she refused to respond in the same spirit. 'What
has happened to ye?' she asked. 'Ye're sweeter, but harder
too. Where will ye go? What do ye intend?'

His smile faded. 'Blood,' he said, calmly but grimly.
'Vengeance.' He stretched, his muscles cracking with the
strain after the long hours in the saddle. 'As ye always
feared, mother.' His smile returned, savage now. Then he
suddenly said, in a rough attempt at reassurance: 'Helen
is no involved. This is matter o' my ain.'

His mother looked at the man beside her, who had gone
away an impulsive boy, with hot and simple notions of
honour. This stern, short-spoken man was bent on some
bitter errand of which he would not speak, which was too
important and close to him for whirling words such as
those he had used in the spring.

'Where will ye go?' she asked again, not expecting an
answer.

But he said: 'To Liddesdale,' and saw her flinch. She
H*

knew as well as any on the Border what that meant. She was silent.

Johnny looked at the crowded hall and the animated faces, grinned at Thomas' awe-struck expression, spoke tenderly to Griselda when she ventured to sit nearer him and take his hand, cracked a joke with Jamie as his brother turned to go back to the store-room. Jamie had heard enough of the quiet conversation to be impressed with his elder brother's new stature; each understood more of the other's mind than he had ever done before.

Johnny's mother suddenly said, startling him with her perception: 'This is o' particular import to ye, Johnny. Ye say that Helen is no involved. If that is so, then ye hae learned to care for some other more than for yourself in these last few months.'

He had turned from the hall to look at her. She was looking down at bread that she had crumbled between nervous fingers on the wooden table.

He watched her in silence for a moment. Then, because she did not press him, because he felt that, in some way, she, of all his family, might best understand, he suddenly said—in a low voice and still somewhat despite himself: 'The minstrel.'

After a short pause in which she remembered all the previous mentions of this minstrel, she nodded. She realised that this explained Johnny's mention of 'we' in the account of his travels. Still she did not look at him; she sensed that he might say more if she did not do so. She only said: 'An' he is dead,' a statement more than a question.

'Aye,' he said shortly. Then, with a rush, telling her more than he had ever thought it possible that he would: 'I must go back. I must revenge him. It was a foul killing. I'll no get out alive, that I ken well enow, but I'll no go down alone. I'll take his killer wi' me, an' any more I can.

I'm no a man o' blood, mother, as ye once thought, but I'm bound to avenge Rainault. This is no undertaken lightly.'

She heard such sadness in his voice that she forgot her own slight nostalgia for her youth, wanted to comfort him but knew that there was no comfort for this loss, and that dissuasion was impossible. Vengeance he must take, she saw, to be at peace with himself, even though it meant certain death. She wondered what kind of boy had so drawn her taciturn son, so committed him? When she looked at him now, he was dreaming, his face bitter. He was seeing a dark valley and a dead man—yet he knew that this was no memory of Rainault.

His mother sat quite still, a trembling of sorrow deep within her. She thought: if he had gone but the once, I could have borne this grief, though I would have known no more of him, nor of Helen. Can I bear it again? She knew she must.

Finally she said quietly, acknowledging his last words: 'So I see, Johnny. So I see.'

She stood up and moved away round the tables, bidding men and women build up the fires, bring more food, and wine. The evening became a festivity at her command. She sent a man out to relieve Jock of his watch and the old man came in thankfully, to rub his hands by the fire and drink a toast cheerfully to Johnny.

His mother toasted Johnny also, with the rest of the company. The household thought they were celebrating his homecoming; Johnny knew that this was his mother's farewell to him. Their eyes met across the crowded hall and each saw in the other's what they had seldom seen or acknowledged before—direct personal love, and a great sadness. A flush filled his mother's usually pale cheeks, giving her the semblance again of the lovely girl she had once been, with a beauty so like that of her eldest son.

Johnny thought sorrowfully: I hae always loved her. But I would hae left her anyway, I could no hae bided here all my life. And now I hae loved Rainault an' to die in avenging his death will be the same as if I had left her while living. Yet he knew that it was not just vengeance for a slain friend that he sought, to satisfy the code of honour of the North, but to strike a blow against evil, that had killed goodness and love.

He let himself wonder, briefly, where he would have been going if Rainault were still alive and had returned with him—back to Nithsdale, to men who seemed more his kin than any Armstrong? or to travel for the sake of travelling, with joy, and with Rainault as his constant companion? The imagined choice touched too near the heart. He dismissed it.

He thought of his mother again; he looked across the hall at her, at the tenderness in her face. He suddenly saw that it was only human affection that softened men's brief, harsh lives. The perception astonished him. He thought, desperately: have I seen it in time? to console her, to let her know that I love her?

He went down into the hall to where his mother stood by the fireplace, and led her back to the high table, with great courtesy. To drown his thoughts, and hers, he toasted her as she had toasted him, but audaciously, openly affectionate, his eyes seeking her tear-filled ones. Was this sufficient? He could not tell.

His forced high spirits during the rest of the evening were hectic, and frightened Griselda after a while. Immediately, he dropped his mask of frivolity and, in turning to comfort his little sister, as he would never have done before, he knew that he had seen the truth of human love and obligations in time, thanks to Rainault, and Helen and Sander, and honourable men and women along the Border.

His mother was smiling at him as he sat with his arm about Griselda. He glanced up and caught her smile, sad as it was; he saw that she knew what he had only just realised, the truth learned from his travels. His answering smile to her was sweeter than she had ever known it.

Epilogue

'Pray for me.'

By the morning, the storm of sleet had blown itself out; instead, the sky lay low and heavy and still above the fells, threatening the first snowfalls of the winter.

In the gloom of first light, Johnny, ready booted and cloaked for his journey, sword at his side, went about the yard with Jamie, seeing the improvements that his brother had made and noticing the well-considered provision for the winter. His praise was curt but sincere. 'Ye're a better farmer than ever I'd hae made, lad,' he said.

Jamie glowed with pleasure. But as Johnny turned towards his horse, his brother suddenly caught him by the arm. ' 'Tis yours still, Johnny,' he said, feeling guilty at his own enjoyment of what Johnny had handed to him, loving his elder brother, knowing where he was bound. 'Dinna gang for me.'

Johnny turned back and smiled into his brother's earnest, urgent face. 'Dinna fret, lad,' he said. 'Ye ken my errand an' that I go on my ain account. An' I go the easier for leaving a good man behind me.' Jamie swallowed, tried to smile back.

The first flakes of snow drifted erratically about the yard as they spoke.

Just before he mounted, Johnny spoke to his mother who had come, unusually for her, to the lower door of the tower. 'When the time comes, mother,' he said, 'an' if she be willing an' he be willing, betrothe Griselda to Wat Henderson. No other. Wat Henderson. He'll be a good man an' she'll be treated well, I ken. 'Twill heal a breach that's a'most mended.'

His mother nodded wordlessly. The inevitability of fate seemed even harder to accept in this dawn. Her son stooped to kiss her, very gently; she clung to him for a moment, felt his arms tighten about her, then loosed him quickly. Both felt the wound of that farewell. Then Griselda came up beside her mother and her anxious little face Johnny kissed, too, before he mounted.

Then he was up and riding to the western gate which Jock held wide for him. His mother and Griselda and Jamie followed through the mire of the yard to watch him go. His mother saw the snow settling and melting on his amber hair and was never to forget that last sight of her son.

'God's blessing on ye, lad,' said Jock, and could say no more. He, also, now knew where Johnny went. Thomas stood by the old man, clenching and re-clenching his fists, his eyes passionate on his eldest brother's face.

Johnny reined in and looked down and round at the pale faces upturned to him in the strange light of that grey dawn. His own face was composed but now his lips twisted a little. Love shook his courage for a moment but then strengthened it also.

'An' on ye all,' he said huskily. Then: 'Pray for me.'

He rode out west, then they saw him turn his horse north towards the Bewcastle Waste again. They watched until the winter haze and the thickening snow hid him from their sight.

Jock, his mouth drawn tight, began to pull the gates to; Thomas helped him, his teeth set into his lower lip. Griselda asked, fearfully: 'Will Johnny no come home this time, mother?'

She, and Thomas also, looked at their elders after this question. Both read the answer in their mother's eyes, in Jock's, in Jamie's. Griselda began to cry silently, tears rolling huge down her pink, pale cheeks.

Her mother took the weeping child by the hand and led her back in a white silence across the yard. The gates clanged shut. Jamie walked slowly across to the byre, his head bent, kicking at stones in his path.

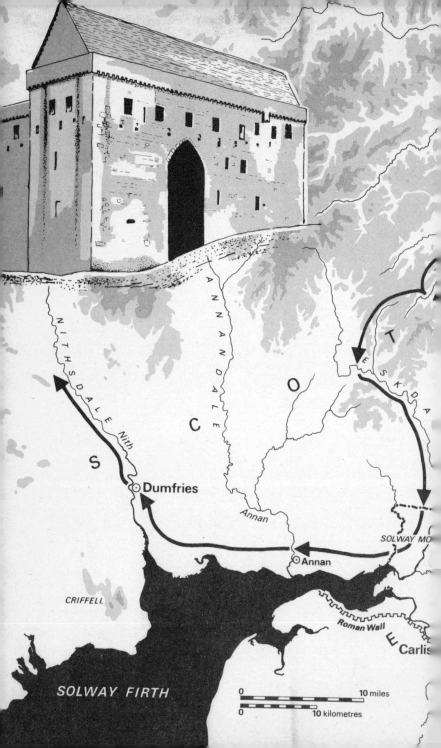

NITHSDALE

Nith

ANNANDALE

SCOT

ESKDA

Dumfries

Annan

S

CRIFFELL

Annan

SOLWAY MO

Roman Wall

E Carlis

SOLWAY FIRTH

0   10 miles

0   10 kilometres